Paddington Children's Hospital

Caring for children—and captivating hearts!

The doctors and nurses of Paddington Children's Hospital are renowned for their expert care of their young patients, no matter the cost. And now, as they face both a heart-wrenching emergency and a dramatic fight to save their hospital, the stakes are higher than ever!

Devoted to their jobs, these talented professionals are about to discover that saving lives can often mean risking your heart…

Available now in the thrilling **Paddington Children's Hospital** miniseries:

Their One Night Baby by Carol Marinelli

Forbidden to the Playboy Surgeon by Fiona Lowe

And coming soon…

Mummy, Nurse…Duchess? by Kate Hardy

Falling for the Foster Mum by Karin Baine

Healing the Sheikh's Heart by Annie O'Neil

A Life-Saving Reunion by Alison Roberts

Dear Reader,

I thoroughly enjoyed writing the opening book for the Paddington Children's Hospital continuity series. The stories are set in a busy London hospital, and it was wonderful to work with other authors and see all the characters come to life.

Though the series is set in London, my hero—Dominic—hails from Edinburgh, which happens to be one of my favourite places in the world. As well as its stunning architecture and history, the people's accent makes my toes curl! This summer I was lucky enough to spend some time in Scotland, and made a little side-trip to Edinburgh with my sister. She accused me of spending a lot of the time daydreaming, and of course I did—I didn't tell her that I was actually rather hoping to run into Dominic.

I hope he makes your toes curl too!

Happy reading,

Carol x

THEIR
ONE NIGHT BABY

BY
CAROL MARINELLI

Published in Great Britain 2017
By Mills & Boon, an imprint of HarperCollins*Publishers*
1 London Bridge Street, London, SE1 9GF

© 2017 Harlequin Books S.A.

Special thanks and acknowledgement are given to Carol Marinelli
for her contribution to the Paddington Children's Hospital series.

ISBN: 978-0-263-06875-7 20405196

Carol Marinelli recently filled in a form asking for her job title. Thrilled to be able to put down her answer, she put 'writer'. Then it asked what Carol did for relaxation and she put down the truth—'writing'. The third question asked for her hobbies. Well, not wanting to look obsessed, she crossed her fingers and answered 'swimming'—but, given that the chlorine in the pool does terrible things to her highlights, I'm sure you can guess the real answer!

Books by Carol Marinelli

Mills & Boon Medical Romance

Desert Prince Docs

Seduced by the Sheikh Surgeon

The Hollywood Hills Clinic

Seduced by the Heart Surgeon

Playboy on Her Christmas List
Their Secret Royal Baby

Mills & Boon Modern Romance

The Sheikh's Baby Scandal
The Innocent's Secret Baby

Visit the Author Profile page
at millsandboon.co.uk for more titles.

CHAPTER ONE

'HELLO, BEAUTIFUL!'

Victoria's smile was friendly as she walked into the lounge ahead of Glen, to where little Penelope Craig, or Penny, as she liked to be known, lay on the sofa. Victoria had already had a conversation with Julia, Penny's mother, in the hallway.

Usually, two paramedics dressed in green overalls entering a home would be a somewhat nerve-racking sight for a six-year-old, but little Penny was more than used to it.

'Victoria!'

Even though she was unwell, little Penny sat up a touch on the sofa where she lay, and her huge grey eyes widened in delight. She was clearly pleased that it was her favourite paramedic who was here to take her to Paddington Children's Hospital, or the Castle as it was more generally known.

'She hoped that it would be you coming to take her,' Julia said.

Victoria gave a friendly smile to Julia and then went to sit on the edge of the sofa to chat to her patient. 'Yes, I was just thinking the other day that I haven't seen you in a while.'

'She's been doing really well,' Julia said.

There was a three-way conversation going on as Victoria gleaned some history from Julia and also checked Penny.

Penelope Craig had been born with a rare congenital heart condition and had spent a lot of her life as a patient at the Castle, but for a while she had been doing well. Her dark hair was tied in braids and she was wearing pyjamas. Over the top of them was a little pink tutu that she wore all the time.

Penny was going to be a ballet dancer one day.

She told that to everyone.

'Your mum said that you've not been feeling very well today?' Victoria said as she checked Penny's pulse.

'I'm nauseous and febrile.'

Whereas most children would say that they felt sick and hot, Penny had spent so much time in medical settings that she knew more than a six-year-old should.

She was indeed febrile and her little heart was beating rapidly when Victoria checked her vital signs.

'She's being admitted straight to the cardiac unit,' Julia said as Victoria checked Penny over. It wasn't an urgent transfer but, given Penny's history, a Mobile Intensive Care Unit had been sent and Victoria was thorough in her assessment.

'Though,' Julia added, 'they want her to have a chest X-ray first in A&E.'

Which might prove a problem.

Accident and Emergency departments didn't like to be used as an admissions hub, though it was a problem Victoria dealt with regularly. In fact, just three days ago she had had an argument with Dominic MacBride, a paediatric trauma surgeon, about the very same thing.

Victoria just hoped he wasn't in A&E this evening, as they tended to clash whenever she brought a patient in.

Generally though, things were better at Paddington's than at most hospitals. The staff were very friendly and there was real communication between departments.

And also, Penny was a little bit of a star!

They'd just have to see how it went.

'I like your earrings,' Penny said when Victoria had finished taking her blood pressure.

'Thank you.'

Usually Victoria wore no jewellery at work. It was impractical, given that she never knew what her day might entail. Her long dark brown hair was tied up in its usual messy bun and, of course, she wore no make-up for work. So yes, her diamond studs stood out a touch.

The earrings had been a gift from her father and Victoria wore them for special occasions. She had been at a function yesterday and had forgotten to take them out.

Penny was ready to be transferred to the hospital. For such a little child, often Glen or Victoria would carry them out, the goal being not to upset them. Once though, Victoria had referred to the stretcher as a throne and Penny, who loved anything to do with fairytales, had decided that she rather liked it.

Penny insisted on moving onto the stretcher herself and Julia took a moment to check that she had all of Penny's favourite things to bring along. They were very used to a 'quick trip' to Paddington's turning into a longer stay.

'Ready for the off?' Victoria asked, and Penny gave her regular thumbs up.

Spring was a little way off just yet, and so even though it was only early in the evening, it was dark outside.

'Are you just starting or finishing?' Julia asked as

Victoria took her seat in the back of the ambulance with them.

'Just finishing,' Victoria said.

'Have you got anything planned for tonight?'

'Not really,' Victoria answered, and turned her focus to Penny.

In fact, Victoria was going out on a date.

A second one.

And she was wondering why she'd agreed to it when the first hadn't been particularly great.

Oh, that's right, she and Glen had been chatting and he had suggested that she expected too much from a first date.

Not that she said any of this to Julia.

Victoria gave nothing away.

She was very discerning in her dealings with people. She was confident yet approachable, friendly but not too much.

The patients didn't mind; in fact, they liked her professionalism.

Socially, she did well, though tended to let others talk about themselves.

Victoria relied on no one.

She and Glen had worked together for two years and it had taken a long time for Victoria to discuss her private life even a little with him. Glen was a family man, with a big moon face that smiled rather than took offence at Victoria's sometimes brusque ways, and he loved to talk. He was happily married to Hayley and they had four hundred children.

Well, four.

But while Glen chatted away about his wife and children and the little details of his day, Victoria didn't.

Certainly she wasn't going to open up to her patient's mother about her love-life.

Or lack of it.

Julia, as she often did, told Penny a story as the ambulance made its way through the Friday rush hour traffic. They weren't using lights and sirens; there was no need to, and Penny was too used to them to want the drama.

'I think it looks like a magical castle,' Penny said as Paddington Children's Hospital came into view.

The Victorian redbrick building was turreted and Victoria found herself smiling at Penny's description.

She had thought the same when she was growing up.

Victoria could remember sitting in the back seat of her father's car as he dashed to get to whatever urgent matter was waiting for him at work.

'That's because it *is* a magical castle,' Victoria said, and Penny smiled.

'It's her second home,' Julia said.

It had been Victoria's second home too.

She knew every corridor and nook. The turret that Penny was gazing at could be accessed from a door behind the patient files in Reception, and had once been Victoria's favourite space.

She would sneak in when no one was looking and climb up the spiral stairs and there she would dance, or dream, or simply play pretend.

On occasion she still did.

Well, no longer did she play pretend, but every now and then Victoria would slip away unnoticed and look out to the view of London that she somehow felt was her own.

'Such a shame they're closing it down.' Julia sighed.

'It's not definite,' Victoria said, though not with conviction. It looked as if the plan to merge Paddington's with Riverside, a large modern hospital on the outskirts of the city, would be going ahead.

There was a quiet protest taking place outside, which had been going for a few days now, with protestors waving their placards to save the hospital.

Victoria's father now worked at Riverside. The only real conversations she had ever had with him were about work. The function she had attended yesterday had been for an award for him, and in a conversation afterwards Victoria had gleaned that it really did seem the merger was going to go ahead.

Of course, the beautiful old Paddington's building was prime real estate.

As always, it came down to money.

'I don't want it to close,' Penny said as they pulled up under the bright lights of the ambulance bay outside Accident and Emergency. 'I feel safe here.'

And Penny's words seemed to twist something inside Victoria.

That was how she had felt as a child whenever she was left here.

Yes, left.

Her father's quick check-in at work often turned into hours but, though alone, and though lonely, here Victoria had always felt safe.

'I don't want it to close,' Penny said again.

'I know that you don't.' Victoria nodded. 'But Riverside is a gorgeous hospital and the staff there are lovely too.'

'It's not the same.' Penny shook her head and there were tears in her grey eyes.

'You don't have to worry about all that now,' Victoria soothed. 'It might not happen.'

She wished she could say it probably wouldn't but it was looking more and more likely with each passing day.

And it mattered.

'Penny!' Karen, a charge nurse, recognised Penny straight away. 'You didn't come all this way just to see me, I hope!'

'No.' Penny gave a little laugh, but just as Victoria went to hand over, Karen was urgently summoned.

'It's fine—we can wait.' Victoria nodded.

They stood in the corridor and made sure that Penny was okay, while Glen chatted with her mother and Victoria started to fill out the required paperwork.

He was there.

She knew it.

And although they clashed, although she had told herself that she hoped he wouldn't be there this evening, Victoria had lied.

She wanted to see him.

Dominic MacBride had been working at Paddington's for a few months.

He was from Edinburgh and that low Scottish brogue had Victoria's toes curl in her heavy boots. Or was it his blue eyes and tousled black hair?

Or was it just him?

She couldn't quite place why she liked Dominic so much. He was crabby with the paramedics and he and Victoria tended to clash.

A lot!

And he was making his way over.

'Here we go,' Glen said under his breath, referring to the argument that Dominic and Victoria had had three days ago.

Victoria was very confident in all her dealings and her assertion seemed to rub Dominic up the wrong way.

He made his way straight over.

'Are you being seen to?' he checked.

'Yes, thanks,' Victoria said. 'Karen's taking care of us. She'll be back shortly.'

Victoria got back to filling in the patient report form but, just as she did, Julia chimed up.

'She's a direct admission but she's just going to have a quick chest X-ray before she goes to the ward.'

'I see.' Dominic nodded and then he came over to where Victoria stood. She could feel him in her space and that he was requiring her attention but she carried on writing her notes, refusing to look up.

His scent was subtle, soapy, musky and male and the faint traces cut through the more familiar hospital scent.

And still she did not look up.

'Could I have a word, please?' he asked.

And now Victoria looked up, quite a long way, in fact, because he was very tall and broad.

He was wearing dark navy scrubs and he needed a shave. He looked as if he had either rolled out of bed or should be about to roll into one and she did her best to stop her thought process there.

'Sure,' Victoria said. She was about to be churlish and add, *In a moment*, and then take said moment to finish her report, but instead she moved away from the stretcher and followed him into a small annexe.

He leant against a sink and she stood in front of him, not quite to attention but she was very ready to walk off.

'Can you not see how busy we are?' Dominic said. 'We don't have time to do the wards' work as well.'

'I don't make the rules.'

'You know them though and your patient is a direct

admission,' Dominic said. 'If she goes up to the ward she can wait in a comfortable bed.'

Victoria said nothing.

They both knew the unofficial consensus was that Penny would be pushed to the front of the X-ray list, just so she could quickly be moved up to the ward.

The annexe was very small.

Dominic was not.

He was tall and broad and his eyes demanded that she look at him; Victoria rose to the challenge and met his angry glare as he spoke.

'I've just come from explaining to a father that there's a three-hour wait for an X-ray. Your arrival has just added to that load.'

'So what would you like me to do?' Victoria asked.

She just threw it back at him because, despite the comfortable bed that Penny would have on the ward, once there she would be shuffled to the bottom of the X-ray pile. It could well be midnight before she was brought down to the Imaging Department.

'It's not just a matter of filling in an X-ray request,' Dominic said. 'She should be examined before she goes around. If anything happens to her without her being seen—'

'So,' Victoria calmly interrupted, 'what would you like me to do?'

She did not engage in small talk; she was confident and assertive and refused to row.

'There you are.' Karen came into the annexe. 'Cubicle four has opened up if you'd like to bring Penny through.'

She and Dominic stared at each other.

The choice was his.

'Fine,' he eventually said, and Karen nodded and went back to Penny.

'Next time...' Dominic warned, but Victoria just shrugged and walked off.

'Victoria!'

She halted.

There was an angry edge to his voice, but that wasn't what stopped her—she didn't think he even knew her name, so his use of it surprised her.

'Don't just shrug and walk off when I'm trying to have a conversation.'

'A pointless one,' Victoria said as she turned around. 'In fact, we had the same conversation three days ago.'

His mood had been just as bloody then and she watched as his eyes shuttered for a moment.

'As I said then, I just go where I'm told and deal with the inevitable angry consequence—I get your ire if I bring the patient here, or the ire of the ward if they arrive without the X-ray.'

She went to walk off, but this time it was Victoria who changed her mind and continued the conversation.

'Sometimes it's made easy though and the staff get that I'm just doing my job. That's generally the case at Paddington's, though I guess it just depends who's on. I have to go and move my patient and then I'm out of here. Which is just as well...'

And then she crossed the line.

For the first time she made it personal. 'Your misery is catching.'

Dominic watched as she swished out of the annexe and he let out a long breath.

They were both right.

There were limited resources and the staff all fought for the charges in their care.

She had rattled him though, not just with her little sign-off comment, but the reminder that they had had this conversation three days ago.

It was a difficult time for Dominic and he was self-aware enough to know he had been less than sunny on that day as well.

And he knew why.

Dominic had always been serious and a bit aloof but he loathed that, of late—Victoria was right—he was miserable.

Not to the patients though.

He shoved his messy personal life aside there.

And then from outside he heard laughter.

Victoria's.

He came out of the annexe and there she was making up the stretcher with her colleague.

'Victoria.'

She turned around. 'Yes.'

'Could I have a word?'

She rolled her eyes but came over. 'Are we really going to do this again?'

'No, I wanted to apologise for earlier.'

'It's fine.'

She didn't need it.

In Victoria's line of work, a small stand-off with a doctor barely merited a thought and she was trying to keep it at that.

But this was a genuine apology and he offered her a small explanation.

'Today's a tough one.'

He offered no more insight but Victoria knew she was hearing the truth.

'Then I hope it gets better,' Victoria said.

'It shan't.'

She gave him a smile and Dominic knew he had lied because it already had got a bit better.

Victoria was stunning.

She was wearing green overalls and heavy black boots and it should have been impossible to look stunning in those, yet she did. Her hair was worn on the top of her head but glossy waves tumbled over her face and her hazel eyes held his.

Yes, she was stunning.

And that was why she annoyed him.

Dominic was not looking to be stunned.

His personal life was very messy and, furthermore, Victoria was far from his type.

She was very direct and he usually liked subtle. He liked women who, well, stayed a bit in the background and didn't demand too much headspace.

And lately Victoria was starting to command a lot of his thoughts.

'I'm sorry too,' she said. 'That bit about you being a misery…well…' She couldn't resist a little play. 'I meant crabby.'

He got her little joke and smiled.

It was not the smile he gave to the patients, because they did not have to fight not to blush, as Victoria was doing. This smile felt as if it had been exclusively designed for her and he was holding her gaze as she completed her apology. 'I went a bit far.'

'That's okay.'

And suddenly things could not go far enough.

There was no way he was going to move things along.

Dominic had a hell of a lot to sort out before he should even consider that.

But…

'I'd offer to apologise properly over a drink but in my current mood I wouldn't foist myself on anyone.'

Foist.

That word made her smile.

First, for the way he said it—his accent was light but very appealing.

And second, because there would be no foisting required.

He was gorgeous, sexy, rugged and, yes, she fancied him like hell. He was older than she usually liked; but then again, Victoria liked few.

She guessed him to be late thirties and she was twenty-nine.

He made her feel like a teenager though.

Dominic made her want to blush, but she steadfastly refused to.

And they kept staring.

'It's fine,' she said again, and then the communication radio on her shoulder started cracking and there was suddenly another voice in the room.

'Victoria!' Glen called, and he must have picked up on the tension as he walked by because he paused.

Thankfully Glen seemed to miss that the tension was of the sexual kind.

'Is everything okay?' he checked.

'Everything's fine,' Dominic said, and walked off.

And everything *was* fine now that he was out away from her gaze. Dominic had been very close to asking her out and now he wanted her gone.

It was that simple.

He did not want anyone closer.

But that did not mean he did not want.

CHAPTER TWO

DOMINIC PICKED UP the patient card and went to check on the new patient before she went down to X-ray.

He was a trauma surgeon and so he found himself working in Accident and Emergency a lot and often pitched in.

'Hey,' he said as he went into the cubicle where the little girl had been placed. 'Penelope, I'm Dominic.'

'Penny,' she confidently corrected him. 'And you're new here.'

'I've been here for nearly six months now.'

'Penny hasn't been an inpatient for ages,' Julia said. 'We've had a good run.'

'Well, that's good to hear.'

The little girl's medical notes were so extensive he could be there till midnight if he read them, but Dominic had caught up on the vitals and Julia was very well versed in her daughter's health.

Penelope Craig had hypoplastic left heart syndrome, or HLHS, a rare congenital defect. She had had surgery as a baby and all her life she had been either an inpatient or outpatient at Paddington's. She had presented a few times with infections and that was the concern now.

Examining Penny, Dominic saw that just from the

minor exertion of sitting forward she became breathless and the slight blue tinge to her lips darkened.

And of course, as Victoria would have well known, it wasn't just a chest X-ray that was required.

Dominic took some bloods as a baseline. Penny would require a nurse escort if she went out of the department for her X-ray. But it wasn't to keep staff levels up that had Dominic call for a portable chest X-ray—he was concerned enough that she was really rather unwell.

And so he paged the on-call cardiologist and asked him to come down and see Penny here rather than waiting until she was on the ward.

It was a locum that he spoke to.

Again.

With the prospect of Paddington's closing down, a lot of the regular staff had gone elsewhere and it was proving difficult to attract new staff when no one really knew if the hospital would even be here next year.

Having spoken to the locum, Dominic went back into cubicle four to inform patient and parent of the new plan.

'Look what Penny just found,' Julia said as Penny lay there holding up an earring.

Dominic didn't need to be told whose it was; he had already noticed that Victoria had been wearing earrings this evening when usually she did not.

He noticed rather too many details about Victoria.

And even her earrings had intrigued him. They were large diamonds, and during their discussions he had been trying very hard not to picture Victoria dressed up to go out.

'It's Victoria's earring,' Penny said to Karen as she came in.

'There it is.' She smiled. 'I've just had a call from

Victoria to ask me to look out for it. You've saved me a job. Good girl, Penny. I'll put it in the safe. Oh, and, Dominic, there's a phone call for you.'

'Take a message, please.'

'It's your father,' Karen said. 'And he says that it's important.'

'Thank you.'

Deliberately Dominic left his mobile phone in his locker at the start of each shift. He did not want his private life intruding on work.

Yet it was about to.

This call was, in fact, three days overdue.

Yes, there was a reason he hadn't been sunny on that day.

The receiver had been left lying on the bench and Dominic hesitated. He let out the tense breath that he was holding on to. He had had months to prepare for this moment and had examined it from many angles, but even as he picked up the receiver, still he hadn't worked out what he would say.

'Hello.' His voice was as abrupt as it had been with Victoria.

'Dominic…' William MacBride cleared his throat before speaking on. 'I'm just calling to let you know that as of an hour ago you're an uncle.'

And still, even with the baby three days overdue, Dominic did not know what to say.

'Dominic?' William prompted.

'Are they well?'

'They're both doing fine.'

Dominic knew that he should ask what Lorna and Jamie had had and whether or not he had a niece or nephew.

He looked out to the busy Emergency Department,

and given it was a children's hospital, of course there were children everywhere. There was Penny, being wheeled over to rhesus for her portable X-ray and in the background there was the sound of babies crying.

Dominic fought daily to save these precious little lives and so, naturally, he should be relieved to hear that mother and baby were well and doing fine.

And somewhere he was.

Yet it was buried deep in a mire of anger and grief, because for a while there he had thought that the baby born today was going to be his.

Dominic tried his best not to recall that first moment of truth—when he had realised the baby that his long-term girlfriend was carrying could not possibly be his.

But then his father spoke of the brother who had caused the second painful moment of truth.

'Jamie's thrilled.'

Dominic held in a derisive snort.

What had taken place wasn't his father's fault. Dominic knew that his parents simply did not know how to handle this.

Who would?

'Will you speak to your brother?'

'I've nothing to say to him.'

A year ago it would have been unfathomable that on the day Jamie became a father Dominic would have nothing to say.

They had always been close.

Dominic had been five when a much wanted second child had been born. Jamie was spoiled and cheeky and always getting himself into trouble, but the rather more serious Dominic had always looked out for him.

Or he had tried to.

Jamie had been run over when he was ten and Dominic was fifteen.

It hadn't been the driver's fault. Jamie simply hadn't looked and had stepped out onto the street and on that occasion Dominic had been too late to haul him back.

It had felt like for ever until the ambulance arrived, and then Dominic had watched the paramedics fight to save his brother's life. Later, at the hospital, as his parents cried and paced, Dominic had gone to try and find out some more. The doors to Resuscitation had opened to let some equipment in and he had seen the medical team in action, doing all that they could to save Jamie.

He had been steered away and sent back to the waiting area but on that terrible day Dominic had decided on his future career.

Jamie had survived and Dominic had really pushed himself to make the grades and get in to study medicine.

Family had been everything to Dominic—right up until the day he had found out that his girlfriend had been cheating on him with his brother, and that the baby Dominic had thought was his had been fathered by Jamie.

Jamie and Lorna had married a couple of months ago.

Dominic had declined his invitation.

Did they really think he was going to stand there dressed in a kilt, smiling for photographers and pretending to family and friends that things were just fine?

No way could he do that.

Not yet anyway.

'We have to move on from this, Dominic,' William said.

'That's why I'm in London,' Dominic responded.

'Because I have moved on.' He went to hang up, yet there was more he had to know. 'What did they have?'

'A wee boy. They've called him—'

'You don't need to tell me,' Dominic interrupted.

'You don't want to know?'

'I already do.'

Dominic was named after his paternal grandfather, as was the Scottish tradition for a firstborn son.

The new baby, if a boy, had always been destined to be called William—whatever brother Lorna happened to be sleeping with that month.

Hell, yes, he was bitter.

'Dominic...' William pushed. He wanted resolution for his family but it would not be happening today.

'I have to get on,' Dominic said.

He didn't.

Dominic's working day was over, but he headed up to the wards, then to ICU to check on a patient.

All was in order.

Only he was in no mood to go home.

That would mean collecting his phone and seeing all the missed messages, as well as spending the night avoiding going online. Oh, he'd blocked Jamie and Lorna ages ago, and his parents weren't on there. But there were cousins and mutual friends, and all would be celebrating.

A baby had been born after all.

'You're very quiet,' Glen commented as he drove them back to the station. 'Did MacBride upset you?'

'Please!' Victoria made a scoffing face and Glen grinned.

He knew firsthand just how tough Victoria was.

And she was.

Men.

She worked alongside them.

And, in her line of work, she saw a lot of them at their worst as the pubs and clubs emptied out at night.

Victoria had seen an awful lot.

She relied on no one and hid her feelings well.

But that tough persona had been formed long before she had chosen her profession.

There had been no choice but to be independent growing up, for there had been no one who had cared to hear her fears and thoughts.

She was outwardly calm and did not get upset about things others might. Even when she realised she had lost an expensive earring, she just checked the ambulance thoroughly and then called Paddington's and asked Karen if she could look out for it.

'You're taking it very well,' Glen commented. 'Hayley would be hysterical.'

'Well, I'm not Hayley.' Victoria shrugged.

Sometimes, she could make life easier playing sweeter, careful of a man's ego.

And sometimes she did.

Like now, as she went into the female changing room to get ready for her date.

She showered and then let down her hair and brushed it so that it shone. Wrapped in a towel she put on some mascara and lip gloss and then pulled on a gorgeous black dress and high shoes.

Sometimes it was nice to dress up, given that she wore overalls for most of her day. But even as she dressed, Victoria knew tonight wasn't going to work out.

He didn't want to hear about her work.

Which wasn't really a good sign, when Victoria worked an awful lot.

As for attraction?

Well, she had rather hoped that might develop.

And that wasn't a good sign, surely.

The condom in her purse would remain unused.

God, it had been ages, Victoria thought, and there was almost an ache for contact and to be close to another, even if just for a little while.

No, her date tonight could in no way deliver the zaps that Dominic's eyes had.

And so she cancelled it.

Right there and then, Victoria pulled her phone out of her purse and told him that she'd changed her mind about going out tonight.

'Another time…?' he went to suggest, but Victoria didn't play games.

'No.'

All dressed up and nowhere to go.

Or nowhere she wanted to be.

She had broken up with someone a few months ago when he had started to make noises about them living together.

No way!

There was no way on earth that Victoria would consider sharing her space with another.

And so she had ended it.

With the same lack of drama as she ended things tonight.

Victoria pulled on her coat and headed out.

'Goodnight,' she called out to her colleagues, but as she walked off Glen called her back.

'Paddington's just called. Your earring is in the A&E safe.'

'Oh.'

'Do you want me to drop you off?' he offered, but Victoria said no. The ambulance station was just a ten-minute walk from Paddington's and, though cold, it was a clear night and she wouldn't mind the walk.

Her heels clipped on the pavement as the familiar building came into view.

Outside were a couple of protestors holding placards with various messages to save the hospital from closure.

They might just as well go home, Victoria thought sadly. From the way her father had spoken there would be a formal announcement soon.

She thought of little Penny's comment about feeling safe there, and that was exactly how Victoria felt as she stepped into the hospital.

There was a feeling that wrapped around her like a blanket, one of being taken care of. There was a sense of security when you were within these walls, Victoria thought as she walked into A&E and saw Karen.

'You're one lucky woman,' Karen said as she made her way over to her. 'Penny found your earring in the blanket. It's locked in the safe in Reception.'

'Thank you so much.' Victoria smiled.

Dominic wasn't here.

She could just tell.

And, Victoria conceded, she was disappointed. She knew that she looked good, and deep down she had hoped that maybe, just maybe, Dominic might revise his suggestion and take her for a drink.

But then what?

She didn't want a relationship. That was the simple truth, and the real reason why she always called things off.

Victoria didn't trust anyone and certainly she didn't

want to get involved with a colleague who she would have to run into day after day.

They walked into Reception and Karen took out the keys and went into the safe, then handed Victoria the slim envelope that contained the earring. As Victoria put it on, Karen started chatting with the receptionist.

'See you!' Victoria called, and went to walk off but then she halted.

She checked that Karen and the receptionist were still talking and realised she could go behind the screen unnoticed.

It was something she had always done as a child and something she still occasionally did, though she always made sure that no one saw her.

Up the steps she went.

Remembering being little, and the hours that she had had to kill.

Growing up, Paddington's had been more of a home than the house where Victoria had lived and she could not stand the thought of it being sold.

She looked out to the night. The moon was huge and she could see the dark shadows of Regent's Park in the distance. There were taxis and buses below and she could see the protestors who, despite a shower of rain, still stood waving their placards.

They didn't want to lose their hospital.

That's what it was.

Theirs.

It was a place that belonged to the people, and now it was about to be sold off and possibly razed to the ground.

Victoria was tough.

She didn't get involved with the patients; she had

made the decision when she started her training to be kind but professional.

But this place, this space, moved her.

The walls held so much history and the air itself tasted of hope. It seemed wrong, simply wrong, that it might go.

There was so much comfort here.

She thought of Penny and how un-scared she was to come to Paddington's.

Victoria had felt the same.

'I shan't be long,' her father would say.

Her mother had left when Victoria was almost one year old and her father had had little choice sometimes but to bring her into work. He would plonk her in a sitting room and one of the staff would always take time to get her a drink or sandwich.

Of course, then their break would end and she would be left alone.

Often Victoria would wander.

Sometimes she would sit in an old quadrangle and read. Other times she would play in the stairwells.

But here was the place she loved most and she had whiled away many hours in this lovely unused room.

Here Victoria would dance or sing or simply imagine.

And maybe she was doing that now, because the door creaked open and she heard his deep voice.

'Excuse me.'

CHAPTER THREE

DOMINIC HAD BEEN about to make his way home after visiting his patients on the wards but, not ready to face it yet, he had decided to spend some time in a place that was starting to become familiar.

He had never expected to see Victoria, yet here she was. Despite the heels and coat and that her hair was down, and despite that he could only see her back and that it was dark, still he recognised her.

But it seemed clear, not just from the location, but from the way her hand rested against the window, and Victoria's pensive stance, that she wanted to be alone.

'Excuse me,' Dominic said, and she turned at the sound of his voice. 'I didn't think anyone was up here.'

'It's fine.' Victoria gave him a thin smile.

'I'll leave you,' he offered, but Victoria shook her head.

'You don't have to do that.'

He walked across the wooden floor and came and joined her at the window.

He was still in scrubs and she could see that he was tired.

'I thought only I knew about this place,' Victoria said. 'It would seem not.'

'I don't think many people know about it,' he said.

'At least, I've never seen anyone up here and it looks pretty undisturbed.'

'How did you find it?'

Dominic didn't answer.

They stood in mutual silence, staring ahead, though not really taking in the view of London at night.

Unlike the thick modern glass in the main hospital, here the windows were thin and there were a couple of cracked ones. The shower had turned to rain and the air was cold but it was incredibly peaceful.

'Where did you work before here?' Victoria asked him.

'Edinburgh.'

'So you're used to wonderful views.'

He thought of the city he loved built around the castle, and of Arthur's Seat rising above the city, and he nodded and then turned his head and looked at something just as beautiful, though he could see that she was sad.

'Are you okay?' he asked, and Victoria was about to nod and say she was fine but changed her mind and gave a small shrug.

'I'm just a bit flat.'

She offered no more than that.

'Has a patient upset you?'

She frowned at the very suggestion and turned to look at him.

'Penny?' he checked, because he had found out this evening that the little girl had wormed her way into a lot of the staff's hearts here at Paddington's. But Victoria shook her head.

'I don't get upset over patients and certainly not over a routine transfer. If I did, then I'd really be in the wrong job!'

'And I doubt it was me that upset you,' he said, and she gave a little laugh.

'No, you I can handle.'

And then Victoria was glad that it was dark because she had started to blush at her own innuendo, even though she hadn't meant it in that way. And so, to swiftly move on from that, she offered more information as to her mood. 'If you must know it's this place that I'm upset about. I can't believe it might be knocked down or turned into apartments. I was practically raised here.'

'You were sick as a child?'

'No! My father worked here in A&E and he used to bring me in with him. Sometimes I'd sneak up here.' She didn't add just how often it had happened. How her childhood had been spent being half-watched by whatever nurse, domestic, secretary, receptionist or whoever was available.

And she certainly didn't mention her mother.

Victoria did all she could never to think, let alone discuss, the woman who had simply upped and walked away.

'My father now works at Riverside—Professor Christie.'

She turned and saw the raise of his eyes.

It wasn't an impressed raise.

Dominic had spoken to him on occasion and knew that Professor Christie wasn't the most pleasant of people.

'He's crabby too,' Victoria said.

And Dominic decided to make one thing very clear. 'At the risk of causing offence, I might be crabby, Victoria, but I'm not cold to the bone.'

Dominic did not cause offence. It was, in fact, rather a relief to hear it voiced as, given her father's status, people tended to praise him rather than criticise, and that had been terribly confusing to a younger Victoria.

It still confused her even now.

She had stood at the award ceremony yesterday hearing all the marvellous things being said about him. Afterwards, at the reception, more praise had been heaped.

The emperor had really had on no clothes, though there was not a person brave enough to voice it.

Until now.

'Well,' Victoria said, 'I saw him yesterday and he seems to think the merge is going to go ahead.'

Dominic nodded; he had heard the same. 'It's a shame.'

'It's more than a *shame*,' Victoria said, and for the first time he heard the sound of her voice when upset—even when they had argued she had remained calm. 'This place is more than just a facility,' Victoria insisted. 'Families feel safe when they know their children are here. It can't just close.'

'Do something about it, then.'

'Me?'

She looked down at the protestors and wondered if she should join them. But in her heart, Victoria knew it wasn't enough and that more needed to be done.

'If you care so much,' Dominic said, 'then fight for what matters to you.'

It did matter to her, Victoria thought.

Paddington's really mattered.

And it was nice to be up here and not alone with her thoughts, but rather to be sharing them with him.

'How *did* you find this room?' Victoria asked again.

He still hadn't told her, and now when he did it came as a surprise.

'I saw you sneak behind the shelves a couple of

months ago and I wondered where you'd gone. When I got a chance I went and had a look for myself.'

'You can't have seen me.' Victoria shook her head at the impossibility of his explanation. 'I always make sure that no one does. Anyway, I'd have known if you were around...' And she halted, because that was admitting that any time she was at this hospital she was aware of where he was.

'I was in the waiting room talking to a parent,' he said. 'I saw you through the glass...'

'I guess I stand out in those green overalls.'

'I don't think it's the green overalls, Victoria.'

She gave a soft laugh.

She was dressed in black now after all.

Yet he was confirming that he noticed her too.

'Did you see me come up tonight?' Victoria asked.

'No. I just wanted some space. I thought you were finished for the night.'

'I am. I was supposed to be going out,' Victoria said, explaining the reason for heels and things. 'But I cancelled.'

And now he thought he knew the real reason she was sad.

'Have you just broken up with someone?'

'I don't think you can really call it a break-up if you cancel a second date.'

No, she wasn't sad about that; Dominic could tell from her dismissive shrug. It would seem it really was just the building.

'Well,' he said. 'I'm sure he's very disappointed.'

And then he went to retract that because it came out wrong, as if he was alluding to how stunning she looked.

'What I meant was that—'

He stopped; whatever way he said it would sound like flirting, and he was avoiding all that.

'I think I've done us both a favour,' Victoria said. 'He didn't seem to understand the concept of shift work. So,' she asked, 'if it wasn't me, then what brought you up here?' She wanted to know more about those difficult days he had alluded to.

'I'm in the middle of something right now...' Dominic said. 'Well, not in the middle—I've taken myself out of the equation. I'm staying back from getting involved with anyone.'

'Good,' Victoria said, 'because I don't like to get involved with anyone at work.'

Yet here they were and the tension that had been in the annexe wrapped and slivered around them.

'Are you married?' she asked.

It was a very specific question and the answer was important to Victoria, because the cold air had turned warm.

'No.'

'Seeing someone?'

'Of course not,' Dominic said, or he would not be doing this—and his hand moved to her cheek. 'You got your earring back.'

'They were a gift from my father.'

'That's nice,' Dominic said.

'Not really, it was just a duty gift when I turned eighteen. Had he bothered to get to know me, then he'd have known that I don't like diamonds.'

'Why not?'

'I don't believe in fairytales and I don't believe in for ever.'

There was, to Victoria's mind, no such thing.

She held her breath as his fingers came to her cheek and lightly brushed the lobe as he examined the stone.

If it were anyone else she would have pushed his hand away.

Anyone else.

Yet she provoked.

'It was the other earring that I lost.'

And he turned her face and his hands went to the other.

This was foolish, both knew.

Neither wanted to get close to someone they had to work alongside but the attraction between them was intense.

Both knew the reason for their rows and terse exchanges; it was physical attraction at its most raw.

'Victoria, I'm in no position to get involved with anyone.'

They were standing looking at each other and his hands were on her cheeks and his fingers were warm on her ears. There was a thrum between them and she knew he was telling her they would go nowhere.

'That's okay.'

And that *was* okay.

'If you don't like diamonds, then what do you like?' he asked. His mouth was so close to hers and though it was cold she could feel the heat in the space between them.

'This.'

Their mouths met and she felt the warm, light pressure and it felt blissful. That musky, soapy scent of him had been imprinted and, this close, it made her dizzy. His tongue sliding in made her move closer and the fingers of one hand reached into her hair as the other hand slid around her waist.

It was almost like setting up to dance, as if the teacher had come in and said, *Place your hands here.* But not.

Because then she hadn't felt a tremble, no matter how warm the palm.

They kissed softly at first as his hand bunched in her hair; he explored with his tongue and it met with hers and he tasted all that had been missing.

Passion coiled them tight; his palm took the weight of her head and pressed her in at the same time.

The pent-up rows and the terse exchanges had been many and could not be dispersed with a single kiss.

It was a deep slow kiss and it birthed impatience in both. He held her head very steady and kissed her hard, and the scratch of his unshaven jaw and the probe of his tongue was sublime. But then, unlike with most men, she tasted resistance.

There was resistance, because Dominic knew very well where they were leading. 'I don't have anything with me,' he said.

And she wanted to feel him unleashed.

'I do.'

And when most would kiss harder, instead Dominic made her burn with his stealth. He stepped back and moved her coat down her shoulders and did not drop it to the dusty floor. Instead he placed it on the window ledge and she went for her purse that was there.

He came up behind her as she rifled through her purse, praying that the condom was still there and trying to find it. One hand wrapped around her and rested on her stomach as his other hand slid up between her inner thighs to the damp in the middle. His fingers stroked her and she closed her eyes to the bliss.

'Here.' She had never been so pleased to find a condom as he peeled her knickers down and she straightened up and stepped out of them.

Still he stood behind her and he lifted her hair and kissed her low on her neck. His hand pressed into her stomach and she could feel him hard against her bottom. Victoria was shaking a little, wanting to turn to him, yet wanting to linger in this bliss.

'Come away from the window,' he said, and took her over to a wall in the shadows and he kissed her hard against it. His hands held her hips and now Victoria felt the delicious hardness of him against her stomach. She stretched up onto tiptoe and he moved his hips down so he met her heat.

It was nice, so nice, to be so raw and open with him.

He caressed her breast through the fabric and, since he could feel no zipper on her dress, with a moan of want he just slid his hand inside and it was the most thorough and deliberate grope of her life. Meanwhile, Victoria was doing the same to him; she was trying to hold on to the condom as she freed him from his scrubs and underwear.

Finally, she held him in her palm, and her hand was soft on skin that was so very firm to her touch.

'I want this dress off...' Dominic gasped, but it was impossible because they could not move their mouths for more than a second from each other.

They wanted nakedness and hours to explore, but their bodies would only give them minutes.

He took the condom and began sheathing himself, while she was pulling up her dress, and when he was done, he lifted her thigh and placed her leg around his hip.

And they were not dancing!

She balanced on one stiletto but his grip of her was

firm and the wall behind her solid. Then her hips angled and both were just as urgent as the other as Dominic thrust and took her.

Victoria had never felt anything so powerful. He was rough and delicious and she felt matched for the first time in her life, because he held nothing back.

Everything he delivered.

Dominic's hand was behind her back and he could feel the scratch of stone on his knuckles but that was so far from his mind that it barely registered.

'There…' she said in a voice that was both demanding and urgent.

He met that demand and heightened it too.

She felt amazing. Dominic was rather more used to holding back, but Victoria invited intensity. It had been ages for Dominic, and he had wanted her for a very long time.

There was almost anger in him for how much she made him want her, so he thrust hard and fast and then harder still to the sound of her pleasurable moans, and then he lifted her.

Victoria had never had both feet off the ground like this; she had never been so consumed. His fingers were digging into her bottom as he took her hard against the wall.

Their faces were side by side and she wanted to find his mouth, but there was no time for that as she was starting to come. Never had she climaxed so deeply, and if she were not wrapped around him she would have folded in two at the pleasure.

He released to her deep shudder and together they hit high, and finally she found his mouth, tasted the cool of his tongue as she drank in his kiss. They rested their foreheads together, sharing those last beats of pleasure and breathing the same air until gently he lowered her down.

With long slow kisses he moved them away from the wall now. She pulled down her dress and then they broke contact and she moved out of the shadows.

Victoria picked up her discarded knickers but had to lean on the ledge, not just so she could put them on, but because her legs were shaky and she was still breathless.

She had never let herself go like that, she had never come so hard and she had certainly never been made love to so thoroughly.

When Dominic emerged from the shadows he, too, was dressed, though his hair was rumpled. It should have been really awkward between them, yet it was not.

'I look like I've been in a fight,' he said as he examined his hands in the moonlight. Victoria took his fingers and looked at them, and made him smile with what she said.

'You're going to have some trouble explaining those injuries, Doctor,' she teased, because it really did look, to her trained eyes, as if he had punched the walls.

Yes, it should have been really awkward but instead he came and sat beside her on the ledge.

'Victoria…' he started, but really he did not know what to say. Dominic was in no position to start anything. And what had just taken place was very far removed from his usual nature.

He felt amazing though, as if on the top of a high mountain.

And she saw him struggle with what to say, so she said it for him.

'You don't have to explain anything,' Victoria said. She was not referring to his knuckles, but still she smiled.

'You're sure?' he checked.

'Yes.'

What had happened was something she could never have imagined, something so far removed from her usual wary approach to intimacy, but he did not need to know all of that.

She felt liberated.

And feminine.

With him she felt she had found herself.

So, instead of an awkward parting they shared a kiss that was deep, long and slow, and ended by her.

'I'm going to go,' Victoria said, and stood.

And still she waited for awkwardness, even as she walked to the door.

So did he, yet awkward did not exist in this room.

'So, if you don't like diamonds,' Dominic called. 'What do you like?'

And she opened the door and laughed as he went back to the original question.

'Pearls.'

He sat in the room and looked around. The moon shone through the window and the air was still stirred and seductive from them; his knuckles were grazed and he was somewhat reeling.

Dominic had never really given pearls any thought before.

They were just something his mother or grandmother wore for weddings and such occasions.

Certainly he had never considered them sexy.

He did now.

CHAPTER FOUR

'PREGNANT?'

Victoria watched as her father took off his glasses and cleaned them. And, as he did so, she remembered the time she had got her first period and it had been almost an identical reaction—slight bemusement, mild irritation, though more at the intrusion of conversation rather than what was actually being said.

Victoria sat in her father's office at Riverside Hospital and waited. For what, she didn't know.

She had read somewhere that some terrible parents made the most wonderful grandparents. That without the responsibility of parenthood, they enjoyed the experience. And she had hoped, truly hoped, that it might be the case here. That this might breathe some life into her relationship with her father.

Apparently not, if his cool reaction was anything to go by.

And Victoria knew deep down that there had been no real relationship with her father. At least, not the sort she wanted. She hadn't seen or spoken to him since the function they had attended, despite Victoria having tried to call.

Her father was brilliant but completely self-absorbed. Completely.

'How far along are you?' he asked.

It had been six weeks since her time with Dominic, and with the requisite two weeks added, Victoria knew her dates.

'Eight weeks,' she said.

'Do you want it?' Professor Christie asked.

He thought she was here to ask for a referral for an abortion, Victoria suddenly realised.

And he'd write her one, Victoria knew.

'Yes,' she said. 'I very much want my baby.'

She stared at him but he was reading through some notes that lay on his desk.

'What about the father?' he asked, and looked up.

'I haven't told him yet. We're not together or anything. He's in Scotland.' Victoria had heard that in passing. 'On annual leave,' she added to her father.

She was forewarned as to the response she might get from Dominic, when her father spoke next.

'Well, he's in for a pleasant surprise when he gets back.'

The sarcasm was evident in his voice and it told Victoria all she needed to know about her father's thoughts on parenthood.

'Victoria, you really need to give this some consideration. Being a single parent is hard work—I should know. It interferes in every aspect of your life. You're the one who always bangs on about your career—think what it will do to that…'

She hadn't seen him since the function and then it had been for an award for *his* career. Victoria didn't bang on, as her father described it. Given he was a professor and specialised in Accident and Emergency and she was a paramedic, she had, on occasion, tried to find some common ground.

But there was none and there never had been.

There was no room in this narcissist's world for anyone other than himself.

'I can't help you financially,' he said, for Professor Christie had amassed a small collection of ex-wives.

'I've never once asked you to.'

Victoria hadn't.

She had left home as soon as she had finished school and had never asked her father for anything.

But she was about to.

She looked at her father and knew that really there was no point even being here. He did not want to be a part of her life, and the occasional public showing of his daughter was only when he was between wives.

'Victoria, I need to get on.'

'There *is* something I want...' Victoria said, and he let out the little hiss of irritation that he always did when she asked for a moment more of his time. 'I was hoping to have the baby at Paddington's.'

Victoria had decided as she'd walked through the corridors of Riverside that she didn't want her baby to be born here. There was nothing wrong with the hospital—she often brought patients here—but it felt bland to Victoria, and her father worked here too.

She felt closer to a building than her own parents. It was sad but true, and that was why she asked the favour.

'They only take complicated cases,' Professor Christie said.

'Not always,' Victoria refuted. And she didn't point out that she'd been born there and that members of staff tended to choose, where possible, to have their child there, but she would not be fobbed off.

'It's closing.'

'Not necessarily,' Victoria said. 'And if it does close

before the baby comes along, then I'll be referred elsewhere, but I'd really like to have my antenatal care
there.'

As an adult she had never asked her father for anything, not one single thing. 'Can you get me in there?'

'I'll see what I can do.'

'Now,' Victoria said, because she knew this conversation would be forgotten the second she walked out of
the door. 'I want to be seen before I tell work.'

And so, more to get rid of the inconvenience, her father made some calls and finally she was booked in to
Paddington's maternity unit.

'You need an ultrasound before he sees you,' Professor Christie said, and he went through the details,
telling her she had an appointment for tomorrow and
that the referral form would be at Reception. Finally,
he asked her to reconsider. 'I really suggest you have a
long hard think about going ahead with this, Victoria.'

That hurt.

On so many levels it hurt.

Victoria knew he had never wanted her. She was
certain that had her mother not left first, then he would
have gone.

As she got to the door Victoria turned and could see
that she was forgotten already—her father was straight
back to work, though she still stood there.

Dominic was right—her father was cold to the bone.

'I can see why she left you,' Victoria said. 'My
mother, I mean.'

Professor Christie looked up from his notes and he
stared at his daughter for a long moment and then, just
before resuming writing his notes, he, as always, had
the last word.

'She left you too.'

* * *

His words shadowed and clung to her right through into the next day.

'You're quiet,' Glen observed as she was driven towards the children's hospital with Glen, for once not in an ambulance.

Glen had offered to come with her for her ultrasound appointment. Victoria had declined, though she was touched that her colleague had given her a lift. She had felt very sick on the underground but that was fading.

Glen knew that she was pregnant.

Of course he did.

He had no idea, though, who the father was.

They worked together, and when Victoria had started to turn as green as her overalls at the smallest thing, he had asked if everything was okay.

Victoria had said she was fine.

Then, a couple of days ago, he had asked outright.

'Hayley had terrible morning sickness, with Ryan,' Glen had told her.

It had been hard to deny a pregnancy when you were sitting holding a kidney dish in the back of an ambulance.

'You have to tell work,' Glen said.

'I know.' Victoria closed her eyes.

It was starting to be real.

For the last couple of weeks she had been in denial, but now she was facing up to things and telling work was something she knew she had to do.

She had this week to get through and then a weekend of nights before she went on two weeks' annual leave and she had decided that she would tell them at the end of her nights.

And now they sat in his car as Glen offered some further advice that she certainly didn't need.

'You have to tell the guy he's going to be a father.'

'Thanks, Glen,' she snapped.

'Listen to me, Victoria—'

'No.' She turned and looked at him. 'I accepted a lift, not a lecture.' And though she told Glen to stay back she knew he was right and that Dominic needed to be told.

When he came back from his leave she would tell him.

If he came back.

He might have decided that he missed home.

Victoria really didn't know him at all.

They had gone straight back to being strangers.

There was no flirting and certainly there had been no reference to what had taken place.

He was still moody and she was her usual confident self.

Really, if it hadn't been for the fact that she was pregnant, by now Victoria would be wondering if it had even taken place.

That night still felt like a dream.

Albeit her favourite one.

'Are you sure you don't want me to come with you?' Glen checked, but Victoria snorted at the suggestion of needing someone to hold her hand.

'For an ultrasound?'

'Hayley gets nervous whenever she has one...' Glen started, referring to his wife, as he always did.

'I'm not Hayley,' Victoria pointed out as she often did. 'I'll be fine on my own.'

She would be better on her own, in fact.

It was what she was used to after all.

Victoria walked through the familiar corridors of Paddington's and turned for the Imaging Department. There she handed over her referral slip to the receptionist.

'We're running a bit behind,' the receptionist explained.

'That's no problem,' Victoria said, even though she was desperate to go to the loo.

She had been told to have a lot to drink prior to the ultrasound so that they might get the best view of the baby.

Still, she had expected to have to wait and had plenty to do.

Apart from a baby, something else had been created that night.

Victoria was on the social committee and had decided to use her position there to start a campaign to save the hospital from the merger.

They met each week over at the Frog and Peach and there was a meeting being held tonight.

It was proving difficult to get things rolling though.

Most people seemed to think it was a foregone conclusion that Paddington's would close. Apart from the odd small write-up in the press, the campaign was not getting any real attention and Victoria was at a bit of a loss as to what to suggest next.

Rosie, a paediatric nurse, along with Robyn, who was Head of Surgery, were both a huge support and Victoria was hoping to catch up with them before the meeting kicked off.

Victoria sent a group text, reminding everyone of the meeting, and then she answered a few emails, but though she was passionate about doing all she could to save the hospital from closure, she could not give it her full attention right now.

She *was* nervous.

Oh, Victoria would never let on to Glen that she was, but she had butterflies fluttering in her chest. She was seated next to a heavily pregnant woman who, from the conversation taking place, was accompanied by her mother.

When Victoria was less than a year old, her mother had decided that motherhood and marriage were not for her and had walked out; Victoria hadn't seen her since.

Not once.

Growing up, she had asked about her, of course. She had craved information, but there had never been much. Her father refused to speak of his first wife and, apart from a couple of photos that Victoria kept to this day in a drawer in her bedside table, she knew very little about her, other than that she had worked at Paddington's.

As Victoria had got older, and she could more readily see her father's very difficult behaviour, Victoria had decided her mother had walked away because she was depressed. A few years ago, Victoria had decided that no mother could walk away like that and have nothing to do with her child.

And so she had to be dead!

It had been a shock and black disappointment to find out that no, her mother was alive and well.

Thriving, in fact, Victoria discovered when she found her on social media.

She lived in Italy with her second husband.

And was a proud mother of two grown-up sons.

Victoria didn't merit a mention.

She had contacted her but there had been no response.

That had been the final hurt and Victoria had decided she would never allow herself to hurt over her mother again.

Yet she was, and today, especially so.

Sitting in the ultrasound department, she was jealous of the stranger that sat beside her.

With her mother by her side.

She tried to focus on an email she was writing on her phone, rather than them. Hearing the doors swish open Victoria moved her legs to let a trolley carrying a patient past.

The child was crying and Victoria looked at him. She was just trying to guess what was wrong with him when she looked up into the eyes of Dominic walking alongside the trolley.

Usually they ignored each other, or spoke only about their patients. Eye contact was pretty much avoided, but today his met hers and she saw that he frowned.

And well he might.

She was sitting in a children's hospital ultrasound waiting room after all!

It hadn't once entered Victoria's head that it might be a problem to see him here today. It wasn't just that she'd thought he was on holiday, more the fact that Victoria was so used to Paddington's, so completely used to being here, that it simply hadn't entered her head that it might be an issue for her to see him.

Yet it had become one.

He couldn't come over—the child on the trolley was very ill—but he turned his head and gave her a questioning look as he walked past.

Victoria didn't quite know what to do.

Dominic was speaking with a nurse and they were about to be shown through to one of the imaging rooms; Victoria wondered if she should go down to Emergency after her ultrasound and speak with him then.

As he steered the trolley he turned and looked at her again but thankfully her phone buzzed and she could legitimately look away.

And, as she did, all thoughts of babies and fathers and ultrasounds rapidly faded.

Major Incident Alert
All available staff are to report to the station.

Sometimes there were mock-ups of major incidents and you were still supposed to attend, so that staff response times could be evaluated. Telephone lines and operators could not be clogged up with calls to check if this was real or not.

And something told Victoria that this was.

She looked up at the television on the wall but there were no breaking news stories yet.

Her phone bleeped again with another urgent alert and Victoria knew that the ultrasound would just have to wait.

Victoria was a terribly practical person and so the first thing she did was go to the ladies' room.

One problem solved.

As she came out, emergency chimes were starting to ring out as Paddington Children's Hospital's own major incident response was set into action.

'Victoria Christie,' she gave her name again to the receptionist. 'I'm a paramedic. I have to go.'

The receptionist nodded. She herself was already

moving into action. If it was indeed a major incident then all non-urgent cases would have to be cancelled, and the department cleared for whatever it was that might be brought in.

'I'll call and reschedule,' Victoria said, and as she went to run off Glen called and said he would meet her at the front.

This was real, Victoria knew, for someone must have rushed to relieve Dominic from his patient because he was running out of the ultrasound department too.

'Do you know what's happening?' she said as he caught up with her.

'No.'

She was very fit but so, too, was he and he passed her.

By the time she reached Accident and Emergency, Dominic was wearing a hard hat and she realised that he was being sent out.

Hard cases were being loaded into the ambulance that would bring him to the scene and Karen was bringing out the precious O-negative blood that was kept in Accident and Emergency for days such as this.

The ambulance station wasn't far from the hospital but Glen, having received the same text as Victoria, had come to collect her.

As she got into the car Glen told her the little that he knew.

'There's a fire at Westbourne Grove,' he said, pulling off as soon as the door closed while Victoria put on her seatbelt. 'It sounds bad.'

Victoria said nothing—she never showed her true feelings, even in the most testing of times—but her heart started to beat fast.

Westbourne Grove was a primary school, and today was a weekday...

'Apparently there are children trapped in the building,' Glen said grimly.

CHAPTER FIVE

EVERY MOMENT MATTERED.

Victoria was well trained to respond to major incidents, and as soon as they were out of the car they ran to get changed.

The station was busy with many vehicles already out at the fire and off-duty staff arriving to provide backup and relief.

She went to the female changing room and took off her jeans and silky rust-coloured top that she had been wearing and then pulled on her overalls and boots. In the main station area she then collected her communication radio and ran out to the Rapid Response vehicle, which Glen was just boarding.

They hit a wall of traffic as soon as they left the station.

Already ambulances, perhaps the first vehicles at the scene, were making their way back to Paddington's with sirens blaring.

It felt as if it was taking for ever to get there.

They had their lights and sirens on but the streets of London were gridlocked. Drivers were moving their vehicles and mounting the kerbs in a bid to try and let the emergency services through.

As well as ambulances there were fire engines, po-

lice cars and emergency response workers on motor-
bikes heading there too, and there was the sound of
many sirens as finally they approached the school.

They could hear the chatter over the airwaves. Children were being dragged out and there were reports of
firefighters going back in over and over again in an effort to reach the ones that were trapped. Most had been
evacuated and, as per protocol, were lined up on the
playground, far from the burning building. The numbers
had to be checked and constantly updated but panicked
parents were also starting to arrive on the scene and
the police were having trouble keeping some of them
back as they desperately wanted to see for themselves
if their own child had made it out.

'Your children don't go to Westbourne Grove?' Victoria checked.

'No,' Glen said. And then he added, 'Thank God!'

The stretch of silence between those words felt like
the loudest part of his response and, Victoria knew,
Glen was picturing just that—his children trapped in
a fire.

A couple of months ago, when they had been called
out to a particularly nasty motor vehicle accident, Glen
had started relating everything back to his own family.
He took it all so personally, and it was getting worse.

Victoria had, on several occasions, warned Glen that
he would soon be on stress leave if he carried on like
this and had suggested that he speak to someone.

Glen insisted that he was fine and that everyone had
their Achilles' heel, and then he had turned it into a
joke. 'Except for you, Victoria.'

That had given her pause, for while Glen's stress levels worried her, Victoria knew that she went the other
way and stuffed down her feelings so that no one, not

even her trusted colleague, could guess what went on inside her head.

Perhaps Glen was right and his responses were more normal, Victoria had reasoned, for there was a part of her that was perhaps a little jealous.

Not just of Glen and his ability to show emotion, but that he was part of a loving family and thought about them all the time, just as they all thought of him. Throughout the day Hayley would call and at night before the children went to bed, if able to, Glen would find the time to call and say goodnight.

'Let's just hope they're all out,' Victoria said as they got their first good look at the scene.

There was smoke billowing into the air, thick and black, as they were waved through the cordons. Some parents were being physically held back, not understanding the chaos they would create if let past.

They were guided to park behind the fire engines and they carried out their stretcher and equipment.

On a playground there were firefighters breathing in oxygen, and lines of children stood crying on a nearby playing field, clearly shocked and scared.

But they were alive and safe.

Some of the more seriously injured children were being treated on the playing field and it was then that she saw Dominic and two paramedics working on a child and draping the little body in saline sheets.

There were constant headcounts of the children taking place by the teachers but, Victoria and Glen were told, it was estimated that there were still two children in the building.

As the burnt child was being moved onto the stretcher a call went up for them to urgently move.

'Stay back.' A fire officer was pushing back the

emergency personnel. 'One of the internal structures is about to collapse.'

They were told that the next casualty, be it child, staff member or firefighter, would be for Victoria and Glen to treat and that for now all they could do was watch and wait.

There was the violent sound of an explosion followed by a deadly silence. And Dominic, who was loading one of the burn victims into an ambulance, turned and looked at the building.

There weren't just children in there; there were firefighters too.

Dominic dealt with trauma daily.

He was trained to the hilt for this and, seeing the child into safe hands, he moved fast to get back to the changing situation.

But as he ran towards the line of emergency personnel, he saw a firefighter emerge, and then, too far to do anything to halt her, he watched as Victoria started to run.

Fury ripped through him at her blatant flaunting of the rules, for it was not only Dominic that called out to her to get back.

But no, she and Glen were moving towards the firefighter and child.

With good reason though.

Victoria took safety very seriously.

They were still being told to stay back, as another explosion could often follow the first, but as practical as she was, Victoria was in the business of saving lives and she could see that this little life was ebbing fast.

The firefighter was struggling, and as Victoria approached he dropped to his knees. She could see that he, too, was injured and had given all he had to get the child out. Victoria knew help was close for him but for now she was more concerned with the child.

It was a little boy and he was bleeding profusely from a neck wound and, as he was laid on the playground, Victoria knew that time was of the essence or he would soon bleed to death. She applied pressure to the wound with her gloved fingers as Glen, who had also ignored the orders to stay back, opened a pack. He passed her some swabs but, though she tried, Victoria could not stop the bleeding. But then she found the spot and Victoria let out a long breath of relief that the bleeding had stopped.

She looked up and saw that Dominic was running over and as he approached he let rip.

'What the hell are you guys doing running forward, when the order was to stay back?'

Victoria shot him a look that said she was a bit too busy to row right now. Dominic dropped down to his knees and his silence agreed to the same as he examined the child.

'It's venous blood,' Victoria said, not moving her fingers. If it had been an artery he would have been dead before the firefighter could get him out but, even so, he was practically exsanguinated.

Glen put oxygen onto the child and Dominic inserted an IV and took blood for cross-matching. He pushed through some IV fluids while calling to Karen to run through the O-negative blood that the Mobile Emergency Unit had brought with them.

It was the most precious commodity in a major incident; O negative is the universal donor and can be given to all without cross-matching. It was used sparingly and Dominic was now grateful for a couple of earlier decisions he had made to withhold some of this most precious resource, believing those patients could wait till they got to the hospital.

This child could not wait.

'We need to get him to Paddington's,' Dominic said. 'Now.'

They were working on him on the playground and Victoria looked up to a colleague. 'Can you bring the vehicle in closer?'

Just as she looked up, Victoria saw that another child was being carried out in the arms of a firefighter. The child had red hair. That was all she could make out—and that the child was limp in the firefighter's arms. Another crew was available to take care of them and so her focus went back to her own patient.

A teacher came over and identified the child that they were working on as Lewis Evans. 'His mother's here. She's frantic.'

'Get the police to take her to the hospital,' Dominic said. 'I'll speak with her there.'

Dominic could see the redheaded child receiving care from a Rapid Response team and a doctor, and his decision was made to leave the scene and escort this patient.

It was a very difficult manoeuvre into the vehicle. Even lifting little Lewis onto the stretcher caused Victoria to lose the pressure point for a few seconds.

It was enough to know that it could not happen again.

Through the streets the ambulance blue-lighted them towards the hospital. The police had the traffic under control now and streets had been closed off so that their return journey was thankfully far speedier.

Victoria's arms ached as she knelt on the floor, and Dominic was calling ahead to Paddington's and explaining he needed a theatre held and the head-and-neck surgeon to meet them in there, when she saw Lewis's eyes flicker.

The blood and oxygen were starting to work.

'Hey, Lewis, you need to stay very still,' Victoria said. 'You're in an ambulance and we're taking you to Paddington Children's Hospital.'

Lewis didn't answer but she spoke on as if he could hear her and her voice was calm and reassuring.

'I'm Victoria,' she told him. 'You're doing so well. I know you are scared and in pain but you're going to be okay. I just need you to stay very still.'

And then she looked up and arched her neck and Dominic offered her some water.

She nodded.

He held her head steady and she took a drink and then Victoria saw the familiar building come into view but she could not relax just yet. Lewis had already lost an awful lot of blood, his heart was beating rapidly and his blood pressure was barely recordable.

'Keep the pressure on,' Dominic told Victoria, and he saw her slight eye roll—she was hardly going to let go!

The stretcher was very carefully lowered so that Victoria could keep the vital pressure sustained.

'That's it...' Dominic said, and someone helped guide her out of the back. Victoria let out a sigh, not quite one of relief, but it was good to be on solid ground and have the patient at Paddington's where he would at least stand a chance.

It was chaos outside the hospital, and security and the police were working together to keep the foyer clear for patient arrivals.

Some parents had headed straight to the hospital in a bid to find out more, as had some reporters. As well as that, there were some people who loved to have a good look at others' misfortune.

It was a relief to step inside.

They didn't turn for A&E, instead they moved swiftly through the corridors, guided by a team leader, and with relief, Victoria saw that an elevator had been held for them.

Theatre was waiting and their efficiency was amazing, so much so, that Dominic raced back down to the Accident and Emergency unit as his skills were still in heavy demand.

It was so calm in the theatre and it was just a blessing to be there.

The head-and-neck surgeon had finished scrubbing and was speaking with the anaesthetist about their approach to the neck wound.

Lewis was being given blood through both arms now and he had been given sedation before they went ahead with the intubation.

And Victoria felt dizzy.

Ignore it, Victoria told herself.

But she had been standing there for what felt like a very long time.

'How much longer?' she asked, because she was starting to see stars.

And whether it had anything to do with her complexion or voice, or just that they were ready now, the theatre nurse took over just in time.

'Come on,' Glen said.

Glen led her out of the theatre and down a corridor and Victoria bent over in the hallway with her hands on her thighs and took some deep breaths, but when that wasn't enough she sat on the floor and pulled her knees up and put her head between them.

'Do we have to go back to the school?' Victoria asked.

'No, we've been stood down,' Glen informed her. 'I'll go and find you some water.'

'Did they get them all out?' Victoria asked as Glen walked off, though she did not look up.

'I believe so,' Glen answered.

He returned a little while later and Victoria took a long, grateful drink as Glen spoke. 'Some have been taken to Riverside but most are here.'

She nodded and, having taken a drink, put her head back down. Victoria wasn't so much dizzy now but re-playing the rescue in her head and questioning her de-cision to dash forward.

It had been instinct, she knew that, but now it was starting to hit home that it wasn't just her own life on the line.

And some time later, that was how Dominic found her.

Slumped against the wall, head between her knees, and Dominic was cross all over again with her for flout-ing the rules and crossing the line.

'How's the redheaded kid?' Glen asked Dominic as he approached.

'I've just brought him up for an urgent head CT and handed him over to Alistair, the neurosurgeon,' Dom-inic said.

He stood over her and she could feel him demand that she meet his eyes.

She looked up then and the look he gave her felt hos-tile, even if his voice was even.

'How bad is he?' Glen asked.

'GCS of six,' Dominic answered Glen while looking at Victoria. 'He was hiding in a cupboard.'

'Poor kid,' Glen said.

It was Glen who asked all the questions, Dominic noted, but he had one of his own, and though it was for the two of them he spoke directly to Victoria.

'Do you always ignore orders? You were told to stay back because a building had the potential to collapse.'

'I could see that the firefighter was struggling,' Victoria explained. 'And that the child was bleeding profusely.'

Victoria was starting to feel a bit better, but she was herself questioning the decision to run forward. She really didn't want to deal with Dominic right now and so she pulled herself to standing and spoke to Glen. 'Let's get back to the vehicle.'

'One moment...'

Victoria turned to the sound of Robyn's voice. Robyn Kelly was Head of Surgery and very much a part of the new drive to save Paddington's.

'Dominic, we need you to speak to the press.'

The hospital had been stretched today but the critically injured were now all in the right place and order was restoring. Speaking to the press after incidents like this was a part of the job and so Dominic nodded.

'And you too,' Robyn said, looking over to Victoria.

'Me?'

'They want a representative from all branches of the first responders,' Robyn explained, and then nodded her head towards a staff room. 'Come and see this.'

The news was on and the cameras were trained on the fire that was still burning but had been brought a little more under control.

And there, in the top right hand of the screen, was an image of Dominic and Victoria bent over little Lewis and together fighting to save his life.

'Angela Marton, a reporter, just asked the viewers to

consider how much more seriously things might have played out if Paddington's had been closed,' Robyn said. 'There are people talking about it all over talkback radio...' She looked over to Victoria. 'Finally there's some anger being generated about the merger.'

'Good,' Victoria said.

'This image is on all the channels...'

Both Dominic and Victoria did their best not to catch each other's responses as Robyn told them that they had just become the poster picture for the campaign to save Paddington's.

Robyn had to get on, and so it was Victoria and Dominic with Glen by their side who walked back through the hospital.

Glen was asking about all the injuries and Dominic was doing his best to reply, but of course his mind wasn't really on the conversation.

It was also moving on from the disaster and back to a few moments before the major incident alert had been put out.

He thought of Victoria sitting in the Imaging Department waiting room, and then he thought of her sitting slumped and pale on the floor outside the theatres.

Anyone would be feeling a bit faint, Dominic told himself. Victoria had been pushing on Lewis's neck for ages.

Then he looked over to her and he could see her staring fixedly ahead.

Once outside they walked over to the press area and Victoria spoke with her supervisor where she was given a brief.

The police would speak first, then the firefighters, followed by Dominic, and then Victoria was to speak briefly about the ambulance response.

'The last child pulled out was Ryan Walker,' she was informed. 'He's six years old.'

'Okay,' Victoria said, and she deliberately did not look over to Glen.

He had a son called Ryan and she knew he would get upset at the link.

She went and took her place in the line-up.

Yes, her mind was busy working out ways to get the angle she wanted included, but she was also acutely aware of the man who now stood next to her.

The cameras were on them as they stood side by side and she could feel his tension.

Though, this time, it was not of the sexual kind!

'We need to talk,' Victoria said as she looked straight ahead. 'Though not here.'

'Obviously,' came Dominic's rather scathing response.

She turned and looked at him, and wasn't sure if he was annoyed that they were going to be forced together as the poster image of Save Paddington's as Robyn had suggested.

Or if, somehow, he knew.

CHAPTER SIX

DOMINIC KNEW.

Or, at least, he was starting to!

He was trying very hard not to believe she might be pregnant by him, and was very determined that history would not repeat itself, and he would not be made a fool of twice.

The press conference went well. Dominic said that it had been a multifaceted effort. Victoria got in her little plug about the potential closure by pointing out that the most urgent cases had needed the proximity of Paddington's to have the best chance for a positive outcome and then they all went their separate ways.

The department was terribly busy and there was soot everywhere and the smell of smoke in the air. As well as injured children, there were staff and firefighters too but, by evening, the department was clearing and they were taken off bypass, which they had been placed on so that they could deal with the sudden influx of patients.

Dominic had been working since seven that morning, and after twelve eventful hours he should perhaps be heading for home.

Instead Dominic showered and changed into black jeans and a shirt and walked over to the Frog and Peach pub where the Save Paddington's meeting was being held tonight.

On arriving, he soon found out that the meeting had been abandoned due to the Westbourne Grove crisis and would be held in a couple of days in a lecture theatre at the hospital.

Tonight, there was too much energy for sensible conversation.

The major incident meant that the staff all needed to unwind and debrief and so it was a very noisy pub that he found himself in.

There was Victoria.

She was wearing the jeans and rust-coloured top that he had seen her wearing at the Imaging Department, and he saw she was chatting with Rosie, one of the paediatric nurses.

And… Victoria was drinking soda water.

Not that that meant anything.

He had no idea if Victoria would normally be having a drink.

The fact was, he knew nothing about her except what had taken place that night.

'Hi, Dominic, how was your holiday?' Rosie asked as he came over.

'Fine,' Dominic said.

'Where did you go?'

'Scotland.'

'Visiting family?' Rosie asked.

Dominic gave a small nod. It was easier to do that than admit that while he had hoped to go and visit his family and let bygones be bygones, he hadn't felt ready.

Dominic didn't even want to attempt another relationship until he had dealt with the rather large items of baggage left over from the previous one. But the thought of asking Victoria out had spurred him on at least to try and so he had headed for home, but in the end he hadn't been able to see it through.

It wasn't that he was being stubborn, more that he was honest and could not simply walk in as if nothing had happened until he had dealt with it in his head.

Dominic wanted a real relationship with his brother and nephew—and yes, Lorna too—and he would not be pushed, for the sake of family peace, into a false one.

So, while he had hoped to visit family and the new baby, the hurt was still there. So he had stayed in a hotel and taken some time to drive around the land that he loved, and in that time he had done a whole lot of thinking.

A lot of his thinking had been about her.

Victoria.

And now she met his eyes.

'We decided not to hold the meeting tonight,' she started to explain. 'We're going to—'

'I already heard,' Dominic said, and when Rosie drifted off to join another conversation, it was just them.

'Do you want to get something to eat?' he offered.

'I've already had something. Do you?'

'No.'

No, he did not want to try and find them a table in a crowded pub. Already Robyn was making her way over, no doubt to discuss how the interviews with the press had gone.

'Come on,' Dominic said to Victoria, because there was no chance of having an uninterrupted conversation here in the pub.

They stepped out into the street but that wasn't the ideal location either.

'We could go to mine,' Victoria offered, but Dominic shook his head.

Given what had happened with Lorna he did not want to get closer to Victoria in the least. He did not want to see where she lived and sit and have a cosy chat. 'There's no need for that,' Dominic said. 'We can say everything we need to here.'

Victoria frowned. 'Are you sure?'

'Quite sure.'

So she went ahead and told him in her usual succinct way. 'I'm eight weeks pregnant.'

And what had taken place between them was six weeks ago, but she guessed, given his qualifications, that she didn't have to tell him that they added on two weeks.

Or maybe she did, because he was giving her a somewhat quizzical look, and so she clarified things in order that there could be no doubt.

'It's yours.'

Dominic said nothing.

What was there to say?

He hadn't even thought to have that discussion with Lorna.

Dominic had trusted his girlfriend completely and look how that had turned out.

How the hell could he even come close to believing someone with whom he'd had sex with on impulse, who carried condoms and who, by her own revelation that night, had just finished with someone else.

No, he would not be fooled twice.

'I've got to reschedule my ultrasound,' Victoria said. 'I wasn't sure if you might want to be present.'

He gave a snort as he recalled the last time he'd been at an ultrasound and all that had transpired then—listening as the doctor gave the dates and asking her to repeat them, then trying to catch Lorna's eyes as she turned away.

And Victoria saw the look he gave and interpreted it correctly. 'I don't need you to hold my hand, Dominic. I meant, I accept it might be hard to believe it is yours but the ultrasound will confirm the dates for you.'

'No, it won't—you say that you're eight weeks pregnant. Well, that means they can only give parameters between five to seven days…'

'Thanks for that.' Victoria sneered at the implication.

'We used protection,' Dominic pointed out.

'I'm not about to try and convince you,' Victoria said. 'I know it's yours but I accept that you might not believe that it is,' she said. 'Whatever way, I felt that you had a right to know and now you do.'

Dominic just stood there, for once unsure what to say. She was as factual and direct as always, but he had been let down so badly before that there was no way he would be letting down his guard again.

He would be keeping his distance until he was certain.

'When the baby is born, arrange for a DNA and, if it's confirmed as mine, then we'll speak about things.'

'That's it?' Victoria checked.

'What else do you want?'

'With that attitude I don't want anything from you,' Victoria said, and walked off.

He watched her hitch up her bag and cross the street, and she was about to disappear into the underground when Dominic found himself running after her.

'Wait!' he called out.

She didn't.

Victoria stepped onto one of the escalators but she

didn't stand and let it carry her down. Instead she walked quickly but knew Dominic was fast and so he caught up with her at the bottom.

'Victoria, wait.'

'No.' It was just as busy here as it had been in the pub and so it was a hopeless place for conversation and, given his attitude, she would not be asking him again to come back to her flat. 'I'm tired, Dominic. It's been a helluva long day and right now I just want to get home and go to bed.'

He could see that she was tired and he thought of the day she had had. And he recalled the anger he had felt when she'd raced forward to grab that child.

No, not anger.

It had been fear that he had felt.

He moved her aside and she stood straight rather than lean against the wall; he put up an arm that buffeted them from the people that passed.

'Have you told work?' Dominic asked, already guessing the answer.

'Not yet,' Victoria said. 'My crewmate knows.'

'Work needs to know.' He thought of her today and the hell of that fire, and not just that—it was a dangerous job indeed. 'Victoria!'

'I'll make that choice,' Victoria said.

It wasn't really a choice; as soon as she knew she was pregnant she should tell them, but Victoria was still unable to get her head around things and had been putting it off.

'Look...' Dominic started, but she shook her head and made to leave.

'I'm not discussing this here. You were the one who chose to be told out on the street.'

He had been.

But to stop her from dashing off he told her some of his truth.

'Do you know how I know about date parameters?'

'Well, you're a doctor...'

'I know about them,' Dominic interrupted, 'because I'd been reading up on things in the baby books. A few months ago I sat in on an ultrasound with my ex and found out that the baby we were expecting couldn't possibly be mine, because I was in India at the time it was conceived. That's why I moved down to London.'

She looked at him, right at him, but instead of a sympathetic response Victoria told Dominic a truth. 'I'm not your ex.'

And then she ducked under his arm and was gone.

CHAPTER SEVEN

No, she certainly wasn't his ex.

Two days later Dominic sat in the back of the lecture theatre and watched as a very efficient Victoria took to the stage.

She was wearing a grey linen dress with flat pumps and her hair was tied in a loose ponytail. She was petite, but her presence was commanding and despite stragglers arriving in the lecture theatre she started the meeting on time.

'Let's get started,' Victoria said. 'It's so good to see such an amazing turnout.'

She paused as someone's phone rang out and, Dominic noted, Victoria was far from shy—instead of putting the person at ease, she glared.

'Can everyone *please* silence their phones?'

'It might be kind of important, Victoria,' someone called out, and Dominic smiled at the smart response, given the people who were in the room.

'Then put it on vibrate,' Victoria said. 'We've got a lot to get through and if we have pagers and phones going off every two minutes we shan't get very far.'

There was a brief pause as a lot of people turned their phones onto silent.

Dominic's was already off.

He had started carrying it at work, though he kept it on silent. He still did not want his personal life intruding. But now, if his parents called, which they quite often did, he would let it go to message, then speak to them during a lull in his day rather than at the end of his shift.

There still wasn't much to talk about. They opted to discuss the weather rather than face the unpalatable topic as to what their youngest son had done.

And, Dominic knew, he had taken out his malaise and mistrust on Victoria.

That was the real reason he was here tonight; he hoped to speak with her afterwards.

For now though, he listened to what she had to say.

Victoria kicked off the meeting. 'The fire has really helped showcase to people how vital an institution the hospital is.'

Robyn's hunch had proven right, and now Victoria and Dominic were the face of the Save Paddington's campaign.

The image of them came up on the screen behind Victoria and she tried not to glance over at Dominic.

He hadn't been at the other meetings, though she now knew he had been on leave. But even if she was glad of the big show tonight and for any support that could be mustered, there was one exception—Victoria rather wished he would stay away, for Dominic was a distraction that she did not need.

Then again, that's what he had done since their night together—distracted her from her life.

Even before that, she had always found herself looking out for him whenever she and Glen brought a patient into the Castle.

'The travel time is a vital point we should make,'

said Matthew McGrory, a burns specialist. He had been working around the clock with the patients from the school fire and looked as if he had barely slept in days. 'Due to the sheer volume of casualties there were some patients that were taken to Riverside, but the most severely injured children came here and were treated quickly. That first hour is vital and a lot of that time would have been lost had Paddington's not been here.'

'Indeed.' Victoria was up-front and well versed. 'And we do need to push travel time and the difference it will make to locals. However, patients come from far and wide for treatment at Paddington's. We need to promote both aspects and we need to start working out how best to do that.'

It was a call to arms meeting.

'The press is onside at the moment,' Robyn said, 'but we need to keep up that momentum.'

Rebecca, a cardiothoracic surgeon who headed the transplant team, spoke about the real issue with doctors leaving and the problems the cardiology department were facing. 'We're only able to recruit on very short-term contracts. Paddington's has always attracted world-class doctors and we can't let that change. The campaign needs to showcase the hospital in its best light.'

Ideas were building and they were starting to run with them; it was decided that the first major event to be held would be a fundraising ball.

The meeting ran for a couple of hours and Dominic watched and listened.

He could only admire Victoria.

From an initial very scattered effort, the drive to save PCH was now starting to come together.

Certainly, with the fire and its aftermath still prominent in the news, the public were starting to understand the real implications of Paddington's closing.

'Right,' Victoria said. 'I think that gives us enough to be going on with for now. Anyone who wants to carry on the discussion can—I think most of us who are not working will be heading over to the Frog and Peach.'

Phones went back on and people started heading out. Dominic made his way over to the stage.

'Well done,' he told her.

Victoria simply ignored him and packed up her computer and things in silence.

She had been on days off since the fire and hadn't seen him since the night she had told him about the baby. She certainly didn't want to see him now.

There was no getting out of it though. Dominic waited till everyone was gone and, when finally they were alone, she turned to face him and hear what he had to say.

'I want to apologise for my reaction the other night,' Dominic said.

She understood it though.

Victoria had sat bristling on the Tube but, even as she had let herself into her flat, she had been able to see where he was coming from. Dominic, especially given what he had been through with his ex, had every right to be suspicious as to whether or not the baby was his, Victoria had decided.

And she was right to hold back, but for reasons of her own that she could not think about right now.

'Dominic,' Victoria said. 'I'm pregnant from our one-night stand. Now, I accept, given what happened between us, you might assume that I drop my knickers like that...' She snapped her fingers. 'But actually

I don't. I broke up with someone before Christmas and since then…'

'I don't need your history. Victoria, I'm thirty-eight. I'm sure we're both going to have had our share of past relationships.'

And that was perhaps the moment she fully realised just how very different they were.

Victoria was twenty-nine and as for relationships…

She hadn't really had any of note.

Oh, there had been a couple of boyfriends who had lasted a few months, but she had never lived with anyone and, in truth, had never really been in love.

'Well, you shouldn't be so sure,' Victoria responded. 'I don't do very well with relationships and so I tend to steer clear of them. As I said, I broke up with someone just before Christmas, and apart from a couple of first dates that went nowhere, there hasn't been anyone since then.' No wonder the condom hadn't been up to much, Victoria thought; it had been in her purse for months. 'This year, apart from one torrid tryst in a turret, there's been no one.' And she smiled at her little tongue twister. 'I believe you were the said torrid tryst.'

'Indeed I was.'

'And I'm sorry your ex cheated and that you're not over her, but that's your issue and—'

'It's not that,' Dominic interrupted.

She raised her eyebrows and Dominic had to concede a smile, because yes, it probably sounded to her as if he wasn't over his ex. He guessed Victoria thought that he had run away to England because of a break-up, so knew he had to explain things a bit better than that. 'The person that Lorna was sleeping with was my brother.'

'Oh,' Victoria said.

And he waited for her to avert her eyes or to do what

everyone else did and move to quickly change the subject, but instead she gave a small grimace.

'Well, that's awkward!'

And he smiled a little and admitted, 'Indeed it is.'

'Are you and your brother close?' Victoria asked.

'We were.'

'And had you been going out with her for long?'

'Yes,' Dominic said.

'Were you living together?'

'Yes.' He nodded but Dominic didn't want all these questions. He was just trying to explain, a little, why he had reacted to the news of her pregnancy in the way that he had. 'I really don't want to discuss it.'

Only that wasn't quite true.

Dominic had discussed it with no one.

Everyone in his family wanted to simply move on from the uncomfortable topic and to act as if nothing had happened. Not Victoria though—she actually made him smile when she spoke next.

'You're *very* good at torrid trysts.'

'It would seem that I am.'

'Were you both sleeping with her at the same time?'

'Victoria!' His voice held a warning. 'I don't want to talk about it.'

'Fair enough.' She shrugged. 'But if that's the case, then I'm going to go for a drink with my committee.'

'Don't we have rather a lot to discuss?'

'I'll be fine,' Victoria said. 'I cope with things. So really, at this stage there's nothing much to talk about. If you want a DNA test once the baby's here, then that's fine too.'

They started to walk down the corridor but as Dominic went straight she turned to the left.

'Where are you going?'

'It's a short cut.'

Dominic didn't want the short cut; he rather liked spending time with her and, though he didn't say that, of course, it was actually nice to be walking and talking.

The short cut was an old quadrangle that he hadn't seen before and there was a glimpse of a navy sky and the scent of fresh air; Dominic guessed it would be a very welcome space to know, if working over a long weekend.

'Maybe it's not such a short cut,' Victoria added as she looked up and felt the cool evening air on her cheeks. 'More, the scenic route.'

'You really do know this hospital like the back of your hand,' Dominic commented. 'Did your father bring you here a lot?'

'Yes, there were a lot of nanny changes and so I'd be brought along until a replacement was found.'

She had been close to a couple of the nannies but they all too soon found it unbearable to work for her father and left.

It had been the same with his girlfriends, who would attempt to win over the daughter to impress the father and then would drop her like a hot stone as soon as the relationship came to an end.

Even when she had been a bit older, Victoria would come here after school or on long weekends, rather than sit in an empty house. Here at the quadrangle, weather permitting, she had done an awful lot of homework!

'What about your mother?' Dominic asked as they started to walk.

'They broke up.' Victoria gave him no more information about her mother than that. She turned and looked at him. 'I shan't let you just drift in and out of my child's life. And I'm not having him or her dropped off here just because you have to work. My baby will be at home with me.'

Dominic said nothing. If Victoria thought he would be a hands-off father, then she was wrong, but Dominic wasn't going to argue about that now.

He had something to ask her. 'I would like to be at the ultrasound.'

But Victoria had been thinking about just that over the last couple of days and immediately she shook her head. 'I don't think so. That offer has been withdrawn.'

'Can I ask why?'

'It just has.'

Dominic knew he didn't have any right to be there and so he chose not to push the issue.

For now.

They were out of the hospital and walking over to the Frog and Peach but suddenly Victoria did not want to go in.

'Are you coming?'

'No.'

She offered no more explanation than that. Victoria didn't need to give him one and was annoyed when Dominic walked after her.

'What?' she asked.

'There's surely more to discuss.'

'I don't see that there is. I'll send you a copy of the images and you can...' She shrugged. 'You can do whatever you're going to do. Measure its little crown rump length and decide if it might possibly be yours.'

Yes, she had read the baby books too.

And she walked off with more purpose this time.

It was all starting to feel terribly real.

For weeks she'd been stuffing down the possibility

that she might be pregnant; now she knew for certain that she was.

But it wasn't just the baby, or telling work that concerned Victoria.

It was Dominic MacBride himself.

She had heard his concern about her working the other night and now she could feel his slight push to be more present; she knew that it was only going to increase.

And she did not want to start relying on him.

She thought of her own mother, who had upped and left, and all the nannies and girlfriends and wives that her father had gone through.

There had been no constant in her life apart from her father and he had merely dragged her to work and palmed her off to others.

No, she did not want to start depending on a man who would no doubt soon lose interest and be gone.

She simply would not do that to her child.

CHAPTER EIGHT

DOMINIC AWOKE TO the sound of sirens in the street below.

In a decisive move, he had bought a three-bedroom apartment close to the hospital and, with the ambulance station nearby, he heard sirens often. Now, each time that he did, Dominic wondered if it might be Victoria's ambulance on its way to something.

She wouldn't even know that she had passed by his apartment, Dominic thought, as Victoria didn't even know where he lived.

They were so removed from each other's lives.

And yet they were not.

Because he thought about her all the time.

He liked her.

Or rather, he was attracted to her enormously and that didn't aide sensible thinking.

Since their liaison at Paddington's Dominic had found himself thinking about her an awful lot.

Prior to that even.

On finding out about Jamie and Lorna he had closed off from others and thrown himself into work.

Absolutely.

It had been his escape from hurt and anger, and the thought of starting again with anyone had been far from Dominic's mind.

But then she had stomped her way into his thoughts with her heavy boots and crisp handovers. Her confident smile had felt like an intrusion, yet he had found himself looking out for her.

Noticing her.

Victoria was a very different woman from any that he was used to liking.

She had intrigued him when Dominic had not wanted to be intrigued, so much so that, even while talking to a parent, he had been aware that she had been stood registering a patient in Reception. He had seen her duck behind the shelves and, later that same day, he himself had done the same and found the place to which she escaped.

And in his time at Paddington's he had escaped there a few times.

Once, when a young life had been lost, he had come from Theatre and told the parents that he had been unable to save their child.

In fact, Victoria and Glen had been the crew who had brought the patient in.

It had been the worst of nights.

His career meant that he was no stranger to death, but while all loss hurt, this one had been particularly painful.

Dominic had raced the little girl to Theatre but she had died on the operating table and telling the parents had been hell.

They had wanted her to be an organ donor and wanted her heart to go to another child.

It was their fervent wish, yet she was already dead.

Dominic had never been more grateful for the appearance of Rebecca in the interview room. She headed the transplant team and Dominic could only admire her empathy for the parents.

She had spoken with them at length and had gone through what *could* be done to give the gift of hope to another child.

Yes, she had empathy because, seeing Dominic, she had said that she would take it from here.

He had lain in the on-call room going over and over the surgery, wondering if there was anything more he could have done, while knowing that the child's fate had been sealed at the moment of impact.

Unable to sleep he had got up and it had been to the turret that he retreated, where he had looked out to a dark London night.

There, away from the constant background hospital noise, he had thought about the doctors who had fought so hard to save his brother, and accepted he had done the same for that child.

There was solace in that quiet space.

And together he and Victoria had found solace again on a very different night—the night that little William had been born.

Every sensible part of him screeched for caution and told Dominic that he could well be being taken for a ride.

Yet the sensible parts did not take into account the magic of that night, the mutual succour, for despite Victoria's denial, despite insisting her pensive mood was reserved only for the loss of the famed institution, Dominic was certain that she had been hurting for other reasons that night too.

He wanted to know Victoria some more.

Baby aside, caution aside, he wanted to know the woman behind the cool façade and it was time to do something about that.

* * *

'You've got an admirer, Victoria!'

She returned from a call-out with Glen to the light teasing of other staff. A large bouquet of gorgeous flowers was waiting for her at the station. There were freesias, which were her favourite, as well as hyacinths and other blooms. They filled the air with a rich sweet scent and all the gorgeous shades of spring were on display.

Though her heart was beating rapidly she did not show it in her expression. In fact, Victoria rolled her eyes as she opened the card, for she was quite certain who they were from.

If Dominic thought that a stunning array of flowers was going to give him a second hearing, and that she would let him in on the ultrasound, then he could not be more wrong.

But then she read the card and found out that no, she was not at the forefront of his thoughts.

'It's from Lewis's parents,' Victoria said, and she smiled as she read it. 'He was the neck injury from the fire at Westbourne Grove.'

'How is he doing?' her line manager asked.

'Apparently he's doing really well and they'll soon be taking him home.'

Victoria only knew that from the card. Unlike Glen, who checked on almost everyone, Victoria chose not to follow up on her patients.

It wasn't that she didn't care; it was more that bad news was unsettling and she had made a conscious choice not to get overly involved.

Lewis's parents had left a present for Glen too—a very nice bottle of wine that he decided would remain in his locker until they had finished nights next week, as on the Monday it would be his and Hayley's wedding anniversary.

Glen chatted about his plans for that night as they drove to their next job. 'Ten years,' Glen said. 'I can't believe it.'

Nor could Victoria envision it! 'So what are you getting her?'

'Hayley says that she doesn't want anything. She just wants…' Glen hesitated and then changed whatever he had been about to say. 'I'm getting her an eternity ring. Sapphire and diamonds.'

'That sounds gorgeous,' Victoria said. 'So what does she really want?' She looked over to Glen, who concentrated on the road ahead, but Victoria could guess exactly what Hayley wanted and Glen knew it.

'Leave it, Victoria.'

Victoria would not.

'How did you pull up after the school fire?' she asked.

'I'm fine. They got everyone out.'

Victoria knew that Glen was stressed. They had been crewmates for two years now. Though it had taken her a while to open up, even a little bit, Glen had been open right from the start.

He was friendly and laid-back and brilliant at his job, but recently things had changed.

They had been called out to a motor vehicle accident a couple of months ago and taken a very sick child to Paddington's, where she had subsequently died.

Some jobs were harder than others and Glen had taken this one very personally indeed. The little girl had been the same age as his daughter and the accident had occurred on a road that his wife often took.

It was a couple of weeks after that that Victoria had

noticed the change in him. Instead of his usual laid-back self, he was tense at times and kept calling home to check with Hayley that everything was okay.

Despite Glen's insistence that he was fine, Victoria was sure that Hayley wanted Glen to speak to one of the counsellors made available to them, but Glen steadfastly refused to do so.

She would wait for her moment, Victoria decided, and, in the meantime, keep a bit of a closer eye on him.

'Your flowers were nice,' Glen said.

'Beautiful,' Victoria agreed.

Which they were, of course, but what was niggling her was that there *had* been a thud of disappointment that the flowers weren't from Dominic and this unsettled her.

It was a busy morning and just as they were starting to think about lunch they were called out to a woman who had collapsed in a shop.

'I haven't got time to go to hospital,' the woman protested as she lay there. Her daughter was with her and was upset, and as they were transferring her mother to the ambulance, they found out that it was her ninth birthday.

'No school today?' Glen asked the little girl.

'She's goes to Westbourne Grove,' her mother said.

Victoria looked over and gave the young girl a smile. 'You're having a bit of a time of it, aren't you?'

The girl nodded. 'My friend Ryan is very sick.'

'That must be so hard for you,' Victoria said.

They took her and her mother to Riverside but once they had settled them in, and just as they were making up the stretcher, Victoria saw her father walking into the department.

He gave her a very cool look. 'Victoria.'

She gave him a small nod back and let out a breath when he had passed.

'Who's that?' Glen asked, but Victoria just gave a noncommittal shrug as if she wasn't really sure who the man who had just passed was.

She wasn't going to tell Glen that it was her father.

Glen chatted about his family all the time and, though it drove Victoria bonkers on occasion, she liked the glimpses of family life and was embarrassed by the state of her own.

They were just starting to think about lunch again when Dispatch asked if they could transfer a patient from Riverside's children's ward to the burns unit at Paddington's.

The burns unit had been stretched to capacity by the fire but a bed had opened up and a very sweet little girl called Amber was, this morning, on her way to join the others at the Castle.

'Hello, Amber,' Victoria said when she met her.

She had a deep burn on her hand, arm and shoulder that was going to require grafting. Amber became teary when she saw the stretcher.

'It's no problem,' Glen said. 'We can take you to the ambulance in a wheelchair if you prefer.'

That seemed to cheer her up and so they fetched a wheelchair and the small problem was solved, but she became distressed again when she saw the ambulance. No doubt Amber was remembering the pain she had been in the last time, and remembered the fear of the lights and sirens.

'I'm going to make you a chicken to keep you company,' Glen said, and Victoria smiled as he pulled out a rubber glove and blew it up.

He was very good with the little children and knew

how to amuse and distract them with antics, such as this one, and Victoria tended to leave that side of things to him.

Soon enough, Amber was holding her 'chicken' and seated in the ambulance, and the transfer went smoothly. As they made their way up to the burns ward she saw Dominic coming down the corridor and walking towards them.

He wasn't in scrubs; he was in a suit and tie and, to Victoria's mind, looked impossibly handsome.

Did she nod and say hi? Victoria wondered, but Dominic dealt with that—he nodded a greeting to them both and Victoria gave a brief smile back.

Glen was a bit cheeky. 'Direct Admission,' he said as they passed. 'We're taking her straight to the ward.'

'That's what I like to see,' Dominic called back.

It was just a little dig, a small exchange, but hearing his voice and dry response made Victoria smile and feel a bit hot in the face.

The burns unit was busy but they made Amber very welcome.

'Hello there.' Matthew, the burns specialist, smiled to Amber as she was wheeled in. 'I'm Matt.'

As Glen and Victoria wheeled Amber into her side room, Matthew had a brief chat with the girl's mother but she soon joined them.

'It's good to be at the Castle,' she admitted, clearly relieved and reassured to be at the famed hospital. 'Amber, you've got a couple of friends here already.'

'It's just like being back at school.' Victoria smiled.

Soon the little girl was settled and they could head off. It was incredibly warm on the burns unit as the temperature was kept high for the patients, but it made for hot work. Victoria would be very glad to get out of there, but first she had a small chat with Matt, who had spoken at the Save Paddington's meeting.

'Still being kept busy?' Victoria asked.

He nodded. 'I don't think that's going to change any time soon. I meant what I said about it being good that the fire happened so close to us. It made all the difference to some of these children. Did you bring in Simon?'

'Simon?' Victoria frowned and then shook her head.

'The little boy from the foster home?' Glen asked, because he knew about all the patients, and Matt nodded.

'No, that was another crew. How's he doing?' Glen asked while Victoria was overheating.

'I need a drink,' she said, and left them to it. Glen would stand chatting for ages and it really was terribly warm in there.

The drinks machine wasn't working but as they passed the canteen Glen nudged her.

'We'll get lunch,' he said.

And she couldn't really protest. There was no stretcher to take back to the vehicle and even if Dominic was in there Victoria knew that she couldn't avoid him all the time.

She just rather hoped that he wasn't there today.

'What do you want?' Glen asked, because they had their routine and usually Victoria would go and get a table while he went and got the food.

Except Dominic was there.

She had known the moment she stepped in, and though she deliberately didn't look over, she was aware that he was seated in the far corner chatting with a woman.

She really didn't want Dominic seeing her alone and

coming over for another 'discussion,' or request to come to the scan.

'Victoria?' Glen checked, because she hadn't answered his question.

'I'm not sure what I want,' Victoria said. 'I'll come with you.'

She chose a salad sandwich and bought a mug of hot chocolate and a bottle of water, as Glen chose tomato soup and a couple of rolls. Together they found a table, thankfully one far away from Dominic.

She drank half her water and then opened up her salad sandwich and took an unenthusiastic bite as Glen slurped his tomato soup.

'Can I ask you something, Victoria?'

'What?' she snapped, awaiting the inevitable questions as to when she was going to tell work, or whether she had told the father.

Glen had asked both regularly since he'd found out.

'Do you put butter on your peanut butter sandwiches?'

Victoria smiled. She liked their often mundane conversations and it helped take her mind off Dominic. 'Of course I do.'

'Well, Hayley doesn't. And apparently Adam has asked that when it's my turn to make the sandwiches, for me not to put any butter on.'

'Adam's nine?' Victoria checked, and Glen nodded and took another slurp of his soup. 'Well, then, I'd suggest he makes it himself if he's going to be so choosy.'

'You haven't tried getting four children to school on time, have you?' Glen sighed. 'If they all made their own sandwiches, aside from the mess that they'd leave behind, they'd never get there.'

And she conceded, because no, she'd never had to get four little people to school before.

But hopefully in a few years she'd have one little person to get there.

The pregnancy was starting to take shape in Victoria's mind and she was beginning to get excited at the prospect of being a mother.

She liked the glimpses of family life that Glen gave her.

It helped her to picture things a bit.

Glen made sandwiches for everyone if he was on an early shift. It gave Hayley a break and it worked well.

Except he'd left his behind today.

Victoria could no more imagine her father making lunch for her than a flight to the moon.

It just hadn't happened.

And they hadn't taken meals together, unless they were out at some function.

'Have you told the guy he's going to be a father yet?' Glen asked, and Victoria sighed. She was just about to tell him to mind his own business when someone answered the question for her.

'Yes, Glen, she has.'

And she stared at her half-eaten sandwich rather than at Dominic, who very calmly took a seat at their table.

'Well, this *is* awkward,' Victoria said.

'Why is it awkward?' Dominic asked. 'All three of us already know you're pregnant.' He looked to Glen. 'Did you know that the father was me?'

'I had an idea that it might be,' Glen admitted, and Victoria threw him an angry look as she realised that he had deliberately steered her into the canteen. Glen picked up his rolls and then stood. 'I'll see you back at the vehicle, Victoria.'

As he walked off Victoria looked over to Dominic. 'I'll be having words with Glen.'

'I wouldn't bother. I was coming by the station tonight to leave a message for you to contact me,' Dominic said.

'Why?'

'Because we need to speak.'

'About what?'

'Well, Glen knows...' Dominic started.

'Glen guessed that I was pregnant,' Victoria interrupted, assuming he was annoyed that others knew.

'Victoria, I'm glad that he knows. It's good that you've got him looking out for you. Mind you, he should have stopped you when there was that fire.'

'Don't interfere with my work,' Victoria said. 'He's my partner, not my line manager. I make my own choices.'

'Fair enough,' Dominic said. He was trying and failing to treat her as he would a colleague. And trying to rationalise that he had every right to be concerned if she was carrying his child.

Only, it wasn't the baby he had been thinking about on that day of the fire, because he hadn't known she was pregnant then.

He had been loading a child into the ambulance and had turned at the sound of the explosion.

He had seen her rush forward towards the firefighter.

Glen had rushed forward too.

And he had seen the firefighters going into the burning building over and over, but it had been Victoria who he had wanted to go and haul back.

Dominic knew already that she wasn't anything like the women he was usually attracted to.

And his response to her was like nothing he had known.

He had just watched her arrive in the canteen a little pink and flustered, though he had soon worked out why when he had watched her gulp down half a bottle of water—they had just come from the burns unit and boots and overalls would not have been the most comfortable things to be wearing.

And he had seen her and Glen, casually chatting as they selected their meals.

He was actually very glad that Glen knew.

'I wasn't going to broadcast the fact you were the father,' Victoria added, 'until the paperwork came in.'

'Who else knows? What about family?' he asked, worried that she had been dealing with this on her own.

'I told my father.'

'And what did he say?'

'Not very much.'

'Is he cross?'

'Cross?' Victoria checked.

'Well, because you're single?'

'I don't think he gives me enough thought to be cross. He was irritated. I asked if he could pull a few strings so that I could have the baby here at Paddington's and he did.' She closed her eyes for a moment. 'Actually, I just ran into him at Riverside.' And she told him what she could not tell even to Glen.

'We hardly even said hello to each other. We had words the other day.'

'About the baby?'

'Sort of.' She gave an uncomfortable shrug.

'I've spoken with your father on occasion,' Dominic told her, and he watched as her eyelids briefly fluttered as he said without words that he got what an awful man he was. When she said nothing he moved the conversation on.

'And your mother?'

'She's not on the scene. I've already told you that.' Victoria took a long drink of her water but then chose to continue. 'That was what my father and I had words about.'

His patience was pleasant; he waited as her eyes scanned his and she wrestled with how much to say. 'He suggested that I think very carefully whether to go ahead with the pregnancy, and that he knew firsthand how difficult it was being a single parent.' Her lips were pale and they clamped for a moment and his eyes still waited. 'He didn't really parent though,' Victoria said.

'Did you say that?'

'No.'

'So what did you say?'

Victoria flicked her eyes away and she gave a tight shrug. 'Nothing.'

And at one-fifteen, in a busy hospital canteen, Dominic knew for certain that he was about to become a father. He knew that because Victoria had just lied.

Something far more had gone on when she'd had words with her father.

And if he could tell when she lied, then the rest was the truth.

'I think,' Victoria said, 'that I'd better get used to the idea that the only person with any enthusiasm for this baby is me.'

And she looked over to him with an angry gaze while her heart waited for him to refute, to say, *No, no, I'm thrilled, Victoria*, but he just looked back at her with an expression that she could not read.

And then she amended that request from her heart

for Dominic to placate her because she wouldn't believe him anyway.

How could he be thrilled to find out that his one-night stand was expecting a baby?

Yet that was what he did—he thrilled.

There was such a pleasure to be had simply sitting here with him. There was such patience in his posture and a measured maturity to him.

Oh, what did he do to her? Victoria wondered, because she had forgotten to look away and still met his eyes.

There was an attraction between them that was so intense it was as if the rest of the people in the canteen had simply faded away.

'Would you like to go out for dinner tonight?' Dominic asked.

'Dinner?' She frowned. She had just stated that no one was very enthusiastic about the baby and he was asking her to bloody dinner. 'What sort of a response is that?'

'A very sensible one,' Dominic said.

He would not lie; he would not feign delight just to appease. 'A date,' Dominic said.

'No!'

'Just dinner,' he added, as if she hadn't turned him down. 'No talk of babies or DNA tests. We can see if we get on, see if we fancy each other.'

And she laughed.

It was such a moot point.

'That's the only thing we've got going for us,' Victoria said.

He liked her assertion.

'I think that's quite a lot to be going on with,' Dominic said. 'For a first date at least.'

CHAPTER NINE

IT WAS QUITE a lot to be going on with!

Victoria had never had this feeling while getting ready for a date.

As soon as her shift was over she raced out of the station and was then chased out by Glen because she'd forgotten to take her flowers.

From there Victoria made a mad dash to the shops where, shame on her, she bought some fresh linen for the bed.

In her defence, Victoria reasoned, she had been meaning to buy some for ages and it was on sale.

Yet, she was pushing it for time and there was one reason only that she was making sure that her bedroom was looking its best!

Yes, she hadn't felt like this in for ever. In fact, it was the first time she had been truly excited to welcome someone into her home.

There was anticipation and a flutter of lovely nerves as she made up the bed, put her flowers into a vase and carried them through to the lounge. She put them on the window ledge and then headed back to the bedroom to choose what to wear. She chose her underwear carefully and then made a dash for the shower.

Dominic pulled up at the flat and, when he buzzed

and was let in, she was still in her dressing gown with wet hair.

'Sorry, we got another call-out just as we were heading back to the station...'

Which was true, but she omitted to mention the mad dash to pretty up her flat.

'It's fine.'

'I shan't be long,' Victoria said.

Her flat was tiny and really very lovely despite its very good view of trains.

It was, Dominic decided as he stood in the lounge, far more straightforward and homelier looking than its owner. There was a two-seater couch and a large chair, which was clearly her favourite, because there was a large ottoman and a pile of magazines beside it; the small shelf was crammed with paramedic procedure manuals.

It was neat but not as fastidiously so as he might have expected; it was very much a working girl's flat.

There was a gorgeous arrangement of flowers in the window and Victoria smiled to herself when she returned to the lounge to find him surreptitiously trying to read the card.

'They're from Lewis's parents,' she told him. 'The neck injury from Westbourne Grove.'

'Good.'

'I don't have a secret admirer.'

'No, you have a blatant one,' he said. 'You look beautiful.'

He made her feel just that.

Whether in boots and baggy green overalls with a messy bun, or dressed up, which tonight she was, he had always made her feel beautiful. This evening she had on a velvety, aubergine-coloured dress and black heels, and her hair was worn loose and down.

'Where are we going?' Victoria asked.

Bed, he wanted to say.

Bed, she hoped he would say.

Yet, there was so much that needed to be sorted first and it would possibly be easier to do that with a table between them.

'There's a nice French restaurant that I've heard about but have never been inclined to try,' Dominic said.

'That sounds lovely.'

Everything sounded lovely with his rich accent. He could have said they were going out for fish and chips and she'd have smiled.

She was putting in her diamond studs and she smiled as she saw him watching.

'They got us into this mess.'

'It's not a mess, Victoria. It's a baby and it will sort.'

But it still felt like a mess to her as she was so jumbled in her head. She wanted his kiss and his touch and to be just a couple going out to dinner, or deciding to hell with it and ringing for pizza later in bed. Yet they were so back to front, and he hadn't wanted to go out with her until he'd known she was pregnant.

It was a hurt that she knew, if they got closer, would only grow along with the baby.

Yes, there was an awful lot to sort out.

'Come on,' he said.

The restaurant was gorgeous and intimate and they were led to a lovely secluded table; it was so small that their knees touched, though neither minded that.

The menu was gorgeous and Victoria groaned when she saw all the lovely cheeses and raw egg sauces that she'd been told to avoid.

'When I'm not pregnant I'm coming here again and having everything on here that I can't have now!'

'Bad choice?' Dominic asked because he hadn't really given the menu a thought beforehand.

'Oh, I'm not complaining.'

She ordered coq au vin and he ordered steak béarnaise. Conversation was awkward at first, but then the food arrived.

'This is delicious,' Victoria said as she tasted her chicken. 'I make it sometimes but mine doesn't come close to this...'

'Well, it wouldn't, would it?'

She looked up. 'Why not?'

'You're not a French chef, Victoria.'

And he made her smile because he stood up to her; he challenged her. 'I could have been, had I put my mind to it—well, apart from the French bit.'

They chatted a little about the campaign to save the hospital and the fundraising ball and then she asked if he missed his old hospital in Scotland.

Dominic paused to think about it. He had been happy where he was, but working at Paddington's he was stretching his skills and really starting to settle in and enjoy it. 'More than I expected to,' he admitted. 'When I left Edinburgh, I wasn't planning on making a career move as such, yet I have. It's a great position and I doubt it would have opened up if there hadn't been the threat of closure.'

'A lot are leaving?'

Dominic nodded. 'They've just recruited a new cardiologist but I know a lot of departments are being held together with locums.'

'Was it hard to leave Edinburgh?'

'Of course,' Dominic said.

'Do you still miss it?'

He didn't really know the answer to that. Going back while on annual leave he had asked himself the same, but the fact was, he was enjoying work and had looked forward to returning to London.

He glanced over to Victoria, who had given up on her main and was waiting for his response. 'In part.'

She was scared to ask which part?

There was so much she wanted to know.

But some conversations were best had over chocolate crepes and vanilla ice cream.

Lorna and Jamie was one of them.

The food was delicious, the topic not so, but they chewed their way through both.

'Did you ever suspect there was something between them?' she asked.

'No, they only met the once…'

He swallowed and carried on.

'Every couple of years I go for a stint of working in India. I first went when I was in medical school and a few of us have kept it going. The week before I was due to go we had a get-together, and Jamie, my brother, came along. Until then he and Lorna had never met. He'd been overseas and had just got back. Well, they got on really well…'

'Clearly!'

She had spent too long chatting on the road to be shocked, Dominic guessed. And it was actually refreshing just to let it out in the open with someone who wasn't shy or coy.

'Apparently they met a few days later by chance.'

'Do you believe that it was by chance?'

She was asking the same questions that Dominic had asked himself. 'No.'

'Does it matter?' Victoria asked.

'It did to me at the time, but no, not so much now.'

And instead of saying he didn't want to speak about it, this lone wolf shared.

Once upon a time, he had discussed things with family. Not everything, of course—Dominic did not readily share his emotions—but for the most part, he and his family would generally talk. About this they could not. His parents wanted to move on and put it aside, to simply act as if it had never happened.

Victoria was the first person he had felt able to explain to about how it had all unfolded.

'When I got back from India, Lorna was throwing up…'

'Tell me about it.' Victoria groaned.

'Do you have morning sickness?'

She nodded. 'It's fading now.'

But they were not here to discuss *their* baby; they were there to find out about each other, and so she was quiet. But Dominic wanted to know how she had been faring.

'Tell me.'

'It's pretty much gone now—I just get really tired. You're keeping me up—I'm usually in bed by eight.' She gave an eye roll. 'And I've got night duty next week.'

He looked at her and there was a twist of guilt that he hadn't been there for her, that Victoria was doing it all on her own.

'Can you change your shifts?'

'I don't roll like that,' Victoria said, and then changed the subject back to what had happened with him. 'So Lorna had it bad?'

'Yes.' He nodded. 'I told her that she was very probably pregnant and she said no, that she couldn't be. I went and got a test and, of course, she was.'

'Were you pleased?'

'I don't know,' he admitted. 'I think so, but it all felt a bit rushed…'

And together they smiled at the irony of *their* situation.

'Lorna wanted to wait before we told our families.'

'I'll bet she did.'

'I told Jamie though,' Dominic said. 'We were always that close.'

'What was he like when you told him?'

'He said congratulations, but not much else.' Dominic shrugged. 'He's always been a lot more the party type than I am. I thought his lukewarm reaction was because he didn't really see becoming a father as anything to get excited over.'

'So you found out at the ultrasound?' Victoria asked, bemused. 'Wouldn't she have known you might work it out there?' It seemed very cruel to have said nothing.

'In fairness to her, Lorna had a bit of spotting so we went to the hospital, and of course they did an ultrasound. For early pregnancy the dating is very accurate. I guessed she'd be nine weeks, but she was six.'

'So you realised then and there?' Victoria asked, understanding a bit better why he had been so opposed at first to attending her ultrasound.

'I did,' Dominic said. 'I asked the doctor to repeat the dates. I honestly thought at first that she must have them wrong, but of course she hadn't.'

'What did you do?'

'We had company at the time,' Dominic answered, referring to the doctor who had been present. 'So I said nothing. Lorna kept looking away when I tried to catch her eye. The doctor said that everything was fine with the baby and when she left we had a talk. Lorna admitted that while I was away she'd met someone. She said she'd been trying to work her way up to telling me, but then when she'd found out she was pregnant, she just didn't know how to, and she wasn't sure, at that stage, whose baby it was.'

'Did she tell you then who the father was?'

'When pressed.'

'Did you suspect?' Victoria asked.

'Not even for a moment,' Dominic said. 'Even when she said that it was Jamie, I was trying to think who we knew by that name. That it must be a colleague or a friend. Even when she said, "Jamie," I didn't straight away think of him. How stupid is that?'

'Not stupid,' Victoria said.

It showed the depth of the breach of trust.

'What did you do?'

'I told her she could take a taxi and I wished her the best—not very politely though. Then I went and met with Jamie. I'd like to say I did the macho thing and we had a fight, but...' He shook his head. 'My brother had a car accident when he was ten. I was there when he nearly died. I just couldn't bring myself...'

And Victoria could see the conflict on his face; she thought of all the bloody, testosterone-fuelled fights she'd seen in her line of work and admired that he'd held back.

'Jamie was crying and carrying on like an overgrown bairn. He said that he loved her, that as soon as they saw the other, they both knew and neither knew what to do.'

And she closed her eyes for a moment, because it wasn't such a torrid tryst after all. It was really rather sad.

'Do you still love her?'

'No.'

Did she believe him? Victoria didn't know.

Did it matter?

Yes.

It did to her. But though bold in her questions about his brother, Victoria wasn't so bold with her heart.

'I said that I'd leave it to him to tell our parents.' Dominic gave a resigned shrug. 'I basically walked out on my life.'

'You've been back though?' Victoria checked.

'No.'

'But you've just been in Scotland.'

'I didn't see my family though.'

And that unnerved her.

It truly did.

That he had walked out on his life, and that even all these months later, they were still estranged.

'What about your parents?' she asked.

'We've spoken on the phone but they just want it to be put to one side. They don't want to discuss it. They just want it forgotten and for things to go back to the way they were.'

'So what were you doing in Scotland?'

'Thinking.'

And so, too, was Victoria.

All she could see was a man who had walked away. 'Weren't you the one who told me to fight for what's important?'

'I'm doing so,' Dominic responded. 'It doesn't have to be with fists.'

'I'm not talking about physically fighting, but they're your family.'

'And I'm doing my best to sort it out, but I'm not a person who just rushes in. I believe that if you say all is forgiven, then you need to mean it. I can't say I'm there yet.'

As Victoria went quiet Dominic called for the bill.

Yet it wasn't just a lull in the conversation, or that the restaurant was near to closing—her silence ran deeper.

As they drove home all she could think of was her mother, turning her back on her own family. Oh, she knew Dominic had far better reasons, but to have completely walked away from everyone he loved, for Victoria it was deeply unsettling.

All the hope of a lovely evening had been left back at the restaurant and Victoria now just wanted to be alone.

'Thanks for a nice night.'

She didn't ask him up and it did not end in a kiss.

Victoria looked at him and all she could see was a man who had abandoned everything he had professed to love.

And so she ended things with her usual lack of flare.

'I'll see you at work.'

'Victoria—'

'Let's just keep it at that,' Victoria said, and when he reached for her arms, she pulled away. 'Please, Dominic, stay back. I want to focus on the pregnancy and I just don't have space right now for anything else.'

That was the longest speech she had ever given to a man when she broke off things, but she knew it wasn't really enough.

Still, he did not push for more explanation and she was grateful for that. A kiss, or attempts at persuasion, would only further confuse her.

Victoria let herself into her flat and the gorgeous scent of freesias greeted her.

She undressed and got into the cold, new sheets and just lay there.

He had loved Lorna, she was sure of that—they had been living together, having a baby together.

Victoria ached for that glimpse of him—she truly did—but knew it was not hers to see.

They were being forced together by default.

She knew he was an honourable man and might want to do the right thing, or at the very least give it a go.

And of course Dominic had said that he no longer loved Lorna, but what if he still did?

What if that was the real reason for leaving Edinburgh so completely?

Victoria had been honest when she'd told Dominic that she didn't know how to make relationships work.

How on earth could this one?

He had only asked her out in the first place because she was pregnant.

What if Lorna decided she had changed her mind? Victoria pondered.

Or what if Victoria gave them a go and then it was Dominic who decided things weren't working out?

Victoria could not stand to fall for him only to be hurt further down the line when later he left.

And he would.

Victoria had nothing in her life to indicate otherwise.

It was safer to face parenthood alone.

She trusted only in herself.

CHAPTER TEN

SHE WAS HER usual confident self at work and did not try to avoid him.

In fact, Victoria met his eyes when she handed over patients and didn't dash off.

Perhaps she actually wanted to be a single parent, Dominic pondered.

Some women did.

He knew that Victoria was incredibly independent and she had told him that she didn't really do well with relationships.

Yet, he wanted a chance for them, and more and more he was getting used to the idea of being a father.

Not in the rush-out-and-buy-the-books way this time.

He was starting to feel the fear.

He saw her leave the department and Dominic followed her out. He knew they would be making up the vehicle and sure enough there were Victoria and Glen.

She was sitting in the back drinking tea poured from a silver flask; it was the only hint that she might be avoiding him, because in months gone by she and Glen would have come into the department to grab a drink.

'How are you?' he asked.

'Fine.' She gave him a smile and Glen made some noise about calling his wife and left them to it.

'When are you on nights?' Dominic asked.

'We start tomorrow.'

'How do you think you'll go?'

'I'll be fine.'

'Well, if you need anything, I'm on call over the weekend, so just—'

'I shan't need anything, Dominic.'

'You do need to tell work,' he said.

Yes, the fear was real and he could not stand the thought of her out on the streets at night over the weekend.

'I know what I need to do.'

She tried to end the conversation but Dominic persisted.

'What happened the other night?' Dominic asked. He had been over and over it, and the night that had started with such promise had failed for reasons that he could not grasp.

'Nothing happened.'

Exactly.

'Just because I'm not talking to my family at the moment, it doesn't mean—'

'Dominic,' Victoria interrupted him. 'What happens between you and your family is your concern. I don't want to get involved with all the ins and outs. I've got enough going on in my own life. Aside from the pregnancy, the campaign for Paddington's is getting bigger by the day.' She gave a shrug.

'What about us?'

'There's no us,' she said, and she made herself look right at him as she did so. 'Dominic, you only asked me out when you knew I was pregnant...' He opened his mouth to speak but she overrode him. 'If I'd wanted anything more than that night, then I think I'm assertive enough that I'd have asked you for a date, but I didn't. We're adults—we'll work things out closer to the baby's due date.'

And still she made herself look at him, though it was almost her undoing because she wanted to lean on him; she wanted him to tell her again that it wasn't a mess.

That it would sort itself out.

She was scared how deep her feelings were for him and was terrified to let Dominic close.

'Have you rescheduled the ultrasound?' he asked.

Victoria nodded. 'It's on Monday at ten. I'll ask them to cc you in on the images.'

'Victoria,' Glen called her. 'We've got a collapsed infant…'

She tipped her drink into the bush and replaced the lid. 'See you.'

It was a call-out to a baby who was unresponsive and the location was a hotel.

Glen drove them right up to the entrance and they loaded their equipment onto the stretcher. A member of staff greeted them and told them what was happening as she showed them up to the hotel room.

'The father called down to Reception and said to get an ambulance straight away and that the baby was very sick,' she explained. 'That's all I really know.'

They took the lift and Victoria looked at Glen, who was very quiet, as had become usual for him when it was children or babies.

The woman who had guided them up knocked on the door and, as she opened it with a swipe card, Victoria stepped in. For the first time in her career, she faltered. A gentleman greeted them in a panicked voice.

'What the hell took so long?'

For an instant she had thought that the man was Dominic.

And in that instant, she told herself that Dominic was way too much on her mind if she was starting to think that complete strangers were him.

This man was younger. It was the accent that had sideswiped her.

And also, Victoria knew, Dominic didn't panic, which this man was clearly doing.

It was all just for an instant, so small that even Glen did not notice her pause.

Just a tiny slice of time, but it was enough for Victoria to realise that this was Dominic's brother.

And so this must be Lorna.

Dominic's ex.

A tearful Lorna was kneeling on the floor beside the bed and bending over her son.

'Why were you so long…?' Jamie persisted.

'Jamie,' Lorna shouted to him to stop. 'He's turned grey! At the hospital we were told he was fine,' Lorna said. 'But I knew though that something was wrong.'

Something was very wrong.

A very small baby was lying on the bed on his back with his limbs flaccid by his side. He wore only a nappy and Victoria could see even before she reached the bed that he was grunting and struggling to breathe.

'Come on, William,' his father cried. He was frantic. 'Come on, son!'

As Glen checked the baby's vitals, Victoria administered oxygen to the infant via a bag and mask. He was breathing, but it was with effort, and so she bagged him a few times, pushing oxygen into his little lungs to assist the little one with his breathing.

As Glen attached him to the cardiac monitor she

could see from the trace and hear from the beeps that his heart was beating far too fast.

'We came down to London to bring him to Paddington's,' Jamie explained. 'My brother is a doctor there.'

And this was no coincidence, Victoria was starting to realise—they had come here to seek help for their baby.

'I know your brother,' Victoria said, and looked up briefly from the struggling infant. 'In fact,' she said to Jamie, though she was too busy to look at him, 'I thought that you were him for a second.'

She felt it better to say she knew Dominic now, rather than to say nothing. There was no time for small talk though; Victoria just felt it was better that she stated it up-front.

The baby had responded to the oxygen and was beginning to pick up; now his little hands were making fists and he was starting to kick at the air.

He went to cry and *that* was the best moment to bag him—Victoria actually saw him pink up before her eyes. In the background, she could hear them explain a little more of what had happened.

'I was feeding him and he just went all floppy,' Lorna explained.

'He's on the breast?' Victoria checked.

'For the most part.' Lorna nodded. 'He had formula yesterday while we were travelling. Sometimes he feeds well, other times it's a struggle, so I've been mixing them up.'

Little William had started to cry in earnest now and was looking a lot better than when they had first arrived.

Victoria and Glen discussed their options for a couple of moments. Inserting an IV would distress him and calling for backup wasn't required yet. Though stable now, he needed to be at the hospital if he deteriorated again, so the decision was made to transfer him as a babe in arms, the priority being to keep him from getting distressed.

They worked swiftly but calmly.

'He'll be more settled if he's held by you,' Victoria explained. As Glen watched the baby, Victoria helped Lorna onto the stretcher. Little William was placed in her arms and the monitor was laid by her legs, and soon they were in the ambulance and on their way to the Castle.

He was pinker now and looked so much better, but Victoria would relay to the staff at Paddington's just how very ill this baby had presented when they had first arrived.

'I've been so worried,' Lorna said. 'I've been saying that there was something wrong with him for weeks and everyone said I was just being neurotic.'

'You're not neurotic,' Victoria said.

Lorna started to cry, for, while it was nice to be believed, it was awful to have it confirmed that there was something very wrong with your child.

'There's been so much going on...' Lorna said.

'It's okay, Lorna,' Jamie said. 'None of this is your fault.' He looked over to Victoria. 'There's been a big family fallout. My wife's been through a lot of late.'

So they had married.

Victoria kept a very close eye on the baby and listened to the couple trying to comfort each other while so very scared for their child.

'Should we ring your parents?' Jamie asked Lorna, and she nodded. 'They're in Greece,' he added to Victoria.

'Maybe we should wait and see what the doctors say?' Lorna suggested.

Little William was a picture of contentment now, pink and warm in his mother's arms, but Victoria's eyes never left him except to glance up and see how far away they still were.

Paddington's came into view, and when there was a very sick child in your care, it was such a sight to see.

That was why so many were fighting to save it.

There were many who knew from painful experience the value of this wonderful establishment.

Little William's arrival was seamlessly dealt with, though the department was clearly very busy.

Victoria knew that even before she stepped inside because there were several ambulances in the foyer when they arrived.

It did not affect the care that William received.

Even though he was pink and crying, Victoria swiftly conveyed that this was rather more urgent than it appeared, more with her eyes than anything else, and the triage was rapid.

They were taken through to the resuscitation area and that was busy too. There must have been a vehicular incident just brought in because most of the bays were full and there was a sense of urgency all around. It was then that she saw him.

Dominic.

He was standing talking to Alistair North, a paediatric neurosurgeon, but he glanced over as Victoria came in.

And then she watched as he looked down to the stretcher and she saw his forehead furrow and his jaw tense at the sight of Lorna holding her small baby.

'Dominic!' Jamie's voice was raw as he called out to his brother. 'He's not at all well.'

And she was right about him—Dominic wasn't one to panic.

He said something to Alistair and then he came straight over.

'William MacBride,' Glen said. 'He became unresponsive while his mother was feeding him...' He relayed some more details as Victoria lifted the baby from his mother's arms and placed William in an examination cot.

'I was going to call you today,' Jamie said to his older brother, 'and ask you to take a look at him.'

'You're in the right place now.' Dominic nodded. He called for assistance, but when there was none forthcoming, he knew that these next few moments were down to him and took command. 'What's been happening?'

'He's been struggling to feed and put on weight. The doctor didn't seem too concerned and the nurse said that Lorna, well...'

'She thinks that I'm overly anxious.' Lorna spoke for herself.

'How was the pregnancy?' Dominic asked.

'It went well.' Lorna just sat on the stretcher, helpless and wringing her hands as her son was transferred from the ambulance's monitor to the hospital's. 'It's just been these past two weeks. We've been getting nowhere. Finally, I got an appointment to see a paediatrician, but it's not for a couple more weeks. In the end Jamie suggested that we bring him down to be seen by you.'

Dominic nodded but did not comment on that—he was too busy taking care of the infant and, despite the pressure he must surely be under, he did not miss a beat. He was feeling the little boy's scalp and checking his fontanelle, which Victoria knew from her own examination was sunken, a sign that he was dehydrated, and Dominic asked for more information.

'So what happened today?' Dominic asked as Victoria helped Lorna from the stretcher.

'We were at the hotel.'

'How long have you been there?'

'We got there around midnight. The journey down was fine and he had a really good night. I was starting to think we were making a fuss to have come all this way. I was feeding him and saying the very same to Jamie when he started to make all these choking noises and he went floppy.' She started to cry and Dominic nodded when Karen suggested that she find someone to take the parents to get a detailed history.

Victoria had helped Lorna from the stretcher and the anxious couple were gently led away, but at the last moment Jamie turned and came back.

'Dominic, he looks fine now, but—'

'I get that he's unwell,' Dominic said. 'Jamie…' His voice was firm. 'You need to hold it together right now. You need to keep your head.'

'I know but—'

'Come on,' Karen said, and he was again led away.

Victoria guessed that it wasn't the first time Dominic had had to tell his brother that.

The baby was listless again—even crying seemed to exhaust him—and while he lay quietly, Dominic had a very long listen to his heart.

And still she stood there.

Glen made up the stretcher and replaced the used equipment, and still she watched as Dominic took blood. Victoria stood outside as a portable chest X-ray was taken.

But then, instead of heading for the ambulance, she went back in.

'Can we get the on-call cardiologist down here,' Dominic instructed.

'Victoria,' Glen called out to her. 'We've got another job to go to.'

She knew that they had to leave.

They were extremely busy, but Victoria found herself wanting to linger and to know more.

She admired how calm Dominic was. Oh, she knew it was his job to be, but no one could even guess what he was going through right now.

There was a sense of agency to him that Victoria liked.

And then he looked up and caught her eyes and she gave a thin smile, one of support, one that said she knew how hard this was.

And he gave back a grim smile of thanks.

'We'd better go,' Glen said.

Only she didn't want to go.

For the first time she wanted to linger—unfortunately, there was no choice but to leave.

It was a long day.

An incredibly long one, and there wasn't a patient aged under sixty in sight, which meant that they didn't get back to Paddington's once.

Oh, how badly Victoria wanted to go to the hospital to find out how William was, but instead they were in and out of Riverside and nursing homes. And in a quick coffee break, where Glen rang Hayley, Victoria thought not just about little William and how he was, and not just about Dominic and how he was coping.

But about Lorna.

Victoria had had neither the time nor the inclination

to think about it when they had been dealing with the baby, but now, pausing for the first time since it had happened, she reflected on the woman that Dominic had once loved.

Perhaps he still did.

In her head Victoria had painted Lorna as some sort of vixen; in fact, she was softly spoken and pretty.

Dominic and Jamie were very similar in appearance.

Jamie, though, was expressive, not just with his emotions but with the information he shared. Oh, she knew the circumstances had been dire today and that people's reactions were often extreme when under pressure, but she just could not imagine Dominic opening up in front of someone else the way that Jamie had.

By Dominic's own admission, even when he had found out the baby wasn't his, he had stayed quiet as a doctor was present.

They were similar, yet different.

And it was the more stoic MacBride brother that Victoria very possibly loved.

It was a scary thought and one she did not want to pursue, but at the end of a very long shift she could take it no more.

'Could we stop by the Castle on the way back to the station?'

'Sure,' Glen said. He could see her tense face and was wise enough not to probe.

It had been a long day for Dominic too.

A new cardiologist had started at Paddington's and Dominic had felt a wash of relief to hand little William over, especially as Dr Thomas Wolfe seemed very thorough, if rather stern.

'He's my nephew.' Dominic had given his findings

and then started to explain the relationship he had with the patient but had immediately been interrupted.

'Then you need to step back,' Thomas had said. 'I'll be in to speak with the family shortly.'

Dominic relayed that information to Jamie and Lorna and though they had communicated throughout the day it had all been about the baby.

Lorna contacted her parents, who were holidaying in Greece, and Dominic was the one who rang his and Jamie's.

They had been very upset by the news and the call had been brief. They had soon rallied though and had called back to say that they were flying down to London and could Dominic meet them at the airport.

The underground would be far easier but their plane came in near the end of his workday and so Dominic agreed. Though he warned that he might be half an hour or so late, depending on traffic.

Then he rang his cleaner and asked her to stop by and give his apartment a quick once-over.

On top of that there were patients, of course, and near the end of a long and difficult day he looked up and there was Victoria walking towards him.

'Do you need me to come out?' he checked, assuming that she wanted him to come and assess a patient in the ambulance, as happened at times.

'No, no,' Victoria said. 'I just stopped by to see how William was doing.'

And he knew from experience that she chose not to get involved with patients, so it touched him that, for his nephew, she had made an exception.

'He's in the catheter lab at the moment. He's had a day of tests and they think he's going to need surgery.'

'Cardiac?' she asked.

'Yes.'

'How are his parents?'

'Exhausted. They're going to be staying with him overnight, of course.'

And tomorrow? she wanted to ask.

Would he be opening his home to them?

But it was not her place to ask such personal questions; Victoria had made very sure of that, so she was vague in her questioning.

'Do your parents know?'

'Of course. They'll be landing in an hour or so,' Dominic said. 'I'll be heading to the airport soon to pick them up.'

'I thought you weren't speaking.'

'We've always spoken,' Dominic said. 'We just didn't know what to talk about for a while.'

And she just looked at him as if he was speaking in a foreign language, and then she gave her smile.

'I've got to go,' Victoria said. 'Glen's waiting.'

'Okay.'

'I hope things go well.'

He watched her walk off, somehow elegant in boots and green overalls, and he did not want it left there. 'Victoria…' he called out, but she carried on walking.

She was, Dominic decided, a complicated lady.

And he wanted to understand her.

CHAPTER ELEVEN

DOMINIC RAN DEEP.

His thoughts he did not readily share and his emotions he kept under wraps.

And it took all that he had within him to keep it like that today.

He was on the phone when Jamie knocked on his office door.

'How is William doing?' Dominic asked.

'A lot better than he was this morning,' Jamie said. 'He's got a hole in his heart and he's going to be reviewed tomorrow by a cardiac surgeon to see if they'll repair it or wait.'

'Well, he's certainly in the right place,' Dominic said.

It was a phrase used often here but it was a heartfelt one and Dominic better understood it now. There was something very special about this place and he could see why Victoria and the others were fighting so hard to save it.

Little William really would get the very best care.

'Lorna can see that now. She didn't want to come down to London given…' Jamie gave a tense shrug. 'I insisted though. I wanted you to take a look at him rather than wait.'

'You did the right thing.' Dominic nodded.

'Look, about—' Jamie said, but Dominic interrupted him.

'Let's just leave it for now.'

'I don't want to leave it though!' Jamie said, his voice becoming distressed as he started to get upset. 'I'm beside myself, Dominic.'

'Listen,' Dominic said. 'For now, you're to focus on Lorna and William. That's it.'

'I need to know that you've got my back.'

'I've always had your back,' Dominic answered. 'You know that I do or you wouldn't have come down to London to have me take a look at William.'

Jamie nodded but he was impatient and wanted resolution. But Dominic would not discuss it today. 'All of that can wait,' Dominic said. 'You need to take care of your wife and son and let nothing else get in the way of that.'

'I know.'

He wanted to tell Jamie that it was time to grow up, but that took things too close to personal and it was everything Dominic knew they had to avoid for now.

'What time do they get in?' Jamie asked.

'Soon,' Dominic said. 'In fact, I need to get to the airport.'

He brought his parents back to the hospital where they fretted for a while, and then somehow the MacBrides did what families do in an emergency—they put differences aside and dealt as best they could with the new hand they had rapidly been dealt.

Most families.

He understood that look now from Victoria.

That brief look where she clearly hadn't understood what he was saying, but he wanted her to understand.

More than that, he wanted to see her.

It was late, he was tired and, yes, he had been told by her to stay back, but instead he found himself at her door.

Victoria opened it and she was wearing the same short white robe that she had been wearing the last time he was here.

She rolled her eyes when she saw him. 'It didn't go well, then?'

'What?' Dominic frowned.

'The family reunion.'

'It went very well, Victoria. I'm just here to see you.'

'Why?' she asked, and then she laughed. 'Stupid question.'

Sex was the last thing on his mind. Well, not quite, but with those three words he knew her a little bit more.

She didn't get relationships.

Not in the least.

'I'm actually here because I've had a crap day and I wanted to see you at the end of it. Are you going to let me in?'

Her flat was dark; clearly she had been about to go to bed but she let him in and turned on a side light.

He took a seat on the sofa and she sat on a chair as if they were in a waiting room.

'How are your parents?' she asked.

'Worried, but they feel better now that they've seen him. They're back at mine.'

'How's the baby?'

'He's on the cardiac unit and he's settled for the night. Lorna's staying with him.'

'Is Jamie back at the hotel?'

'No, he's staying at mine too.' He saw her eyes widen a fraction and chose to explain how it had come about. 'Jamie didn't know the way to the underground, nor about Oyster cards and things, so I offered to drop him off at the hotel. In the end I said to just check out and to come and stay at mine.'

'Are you two talking, then?'

'A bit,' he said, and then admitted more. 'Not really.'

'Then how come he's staying at yours?'

'Because he's my brother and his baby is sick, and right now the baby is the priority. The rest will have to wait.'

His voice was brusque, though he hadn't meant it to be. 'Sorry.'

'No, no...' Victoria said.

It really had been a difficult day.

'Thomas seems to think he might need surgery.'

'Thomas?' Victoria checked.

'Thomas Wolfe. He's a new cardiologist.'

'He's not new,' Victoria said, and shook her head.

'Yes, he is. He only just started at Paddington's the other day.'

'No, he used to work there years ago when I first started. He's a lovely guy.'

Dominic didn't comment; lovely wasn't how he'd describe any guy, but certainly it was not a word he'd expect to hear to describe Thomas, who he had found rather stand-offish.

Still, he didn't dwell on it.

He took in a breath and closed his eyes. It was the first time he had properly paused since he had looked up and seen Victoria walking towards him with Jamie by her side and Lorna and William on the stretcher.

'Jamie was going to call and ask me to take a look at him this afternoon...'

'I know that.'

And it was then she knew for certain that she loved him.

She didn't even have to ask what his response to that phone call would have been.

And yes, while she wanted happy reunions and for him to say that his family was fine, she was starting to understand that Dominic did not say what you wanted him to. He spoke the truth.

Having seen Lorna and Jamie for herself, she was starting to comprehend the magnitude of the betrayal.

It was a miracle, really, that Dominic had followed her into the underground that night when she had first told him she was pregnant, and that he kept coming back when so many men would have turned away.

She wanted to ask him about Lorna, how it had felt to see her today after all this time, but she knew that wasn't needed now.

'Jamie tried to talk about it,' Dominic admitted. 'But I told him that for now he has to focus on the baby. I am trying to work on things with my family, Victoria,' he said. 'But I need to do it at my own pace, not theirs.'

'I know that,' she said. 'But how can you sort it out living so far apart?'

'Because I couldn't work on it from there. Victoria, families fall out. You yourself said you've had words with your father…'

'Your family wants you to be in their lives though.'

'Doesn't he?'

'He wants me there to attend functions when he's between wives.'

'What was the row about between you?'

'I told you,' she said, but she knew she hadn't properly. 'I said I could see why my mother left him.'

'And what did he say to that?'

She shrugged.

Victoria simply wasn't ready to go there.

'Do you want a drink?' she offered.

'I do, but I have to drive.'

'I meant tea.'

'No thanks, then.'

She stood up to get him a Scotch or whatever she had to hand. 'Have a drink. I can drive you home.'

'No thanks,' he said. 'I need the car in case something happens overnight.'

She stood still. There were other solutions and both of them mentally explored them. Dominic wanted her to come back to his—he needed her tonight—but his family were all there and so he could not suggest that.

And though he wanted to stay here a while, both knew where that could lead.

Would lead.

He could see her nipples protruding through the dressing gown—life would be far less complicated if they did not so completely turn each other on.

But no, he could not stay here for the night.

'I really do need to get back home. I just wanted to stop by and tell you what was happening.'

It was nice that he had stopped by, Victoria thought, for she had been fretting about it all evening. It didn't really make sense to Victoria—after all, she had been to the hospital to see how the baby was, but she had just felt a bit sick about little William since the moment she had realised that the baby they had been called out to was Dominic's nephew.

'Will your parents worry if I keep you out late?' Victoria teased, and he rolled his eyes.

'My mother asked where I was going at this time of the night. They're driving me crazy already.'

And she smiled because it was said without malice. He put out his hand and when she took it he pulled her onto his lap.

'How are they driving you crazy?'

'Because in the twenty years that I haven't lived at home, nothing has changed. They hadn't had dinner and I suggested that we get a takeaway, as you do. But no, she wanted us all to sit down and have a proper dinner, as she calls it.'

Victoria found that her smile widened.

Oh, she loved glimpses of family life.

'Well,' Dominic continued, 'I don't really have the ingredients for a proper dinner in my kitchen, so I said I'd go shopping and of course that meant she had to come with me...'

And he was smiling now as he told her about the little shopping trip. 'Do you know how many different types of potatoes there are? Well, I do now. And for all the potatoes in the supermarket they didn't have the ones she preferred.'

'Of course they didn't.'

He let out a soft laugh and then looked to the woman on his lap and Victoria looked back at him.

She felt his hand around her waist and the warmth of his palm through the fabric. 'I'm sorry it's been such a bad day,' Victoria said.

'It's not now.'

The world and its problems were outside and waiting and he would give them all the attention that was needed. But right here, right now, the night felt kinder than the day.

'I do have to go...' he told her.

'I know that you do,' Victoria said, but she did not move from his lap and he made no move to stand.

He looked at her hair which tumbled down over her shoulders and he knew that she wore nothing beneath the robe. He looked at her mouth and then back to her eyes.

A train rattled past which told her the time. She actually liked the sound—it was like having an erratic cuckoo clock in her home but, Victoria knew, this train was the last of the night and she would not hear that sound again until just after five.

And what would her life be like then?

More complicated, Victoria was sure, because it was she who moved in for his mouth.

She tasted resistance—oh, yes, she did—for Dominic had not come here for that and did not want to muddy the waters...while, of course, also desperately wanting to.

For muddied waters became crystal clear as he tasted her kiss and it was all terribly simple after that. It had been a day of holding back and he could sustain it no more, for today *had* been hellish and now the night was not just kind, it was inviting.

Escape beckoned and he drew her in closer, hitching her up on his lap while his hands went into her hair. But Victoria pulled them down, for this was her kiss to him. And so she turned in his lap and straddled him so his hands were free to roam her.

And then he kissed her lazily as she rose on her knees to him, a kiss that simply let her lead and gladly she did. Victoria explored his mouth at her leisure as he ran his hands over her bottom and then released the tie on her robe so that it fell open.

Now his mouth was more urgent as they explored with their tongues and she knew she had never enjoyed kissing more than she did with him.

It was hungry and teasing and they shared moans of pleasure, and as his hands toyed with her breasts she was raw with need for him.

The kiss went deeper and he pulled her higher on his thighs so that she could feel him hard at her centre. She was holding his face in her hands as she kissed him and he ground her down on him.

Then she lifted higher so that he could taste her breast with warm licks, and when he pulled his mouth away, the sudden loss made her crave more.

Victoria had never wanted anyone as badly as she wanted him.

She had missed his touch and now, when there was so much to sort out, they sought the one thing that was already clear—a mutual and very deep want.

'Please...' she said while making room for his hands to free himself. Victoria could feel his breath on her breast as she held on to his shoulders. But when she could simply have lowered herself onto him, instead he ran his hand up her inner thigh and then played with her for a moment, sliding his fingers inside till she was quivering. But she did not have to ask twice for him to take her.

He eased himself inside her as she lowered herself down, and he swore with the bliss of her tight grip and told himself to hold on.

Victoria now wanted his skin pressed to hers. It seemed cruel that he was dressed, but she was so hot in his arms that all she could manage was a couple of buttons on his shirt before she gave up trying to open it.

He thrust upwards while pulling her down and the feel of him so deep inside her almost shot her into orbit.

It was raw and fast and there were hungry kisses in between, and then he turned his head to halt their kiss and slid his hips forward in the chair, taking her with him and allowing him to watch their union.

Victoria still held his shoulders and she, too, looked down. He lifted her hips and held her at his tip, then thrust just a little and the pleasure drove them both wild. She could not sustain it as she was starting to come so he pulled her hard down. She tightened and pulsed around him as Dominic came to her body's command. Relishing the heat of release, she rested on his shoulder, gathering her breath, while he moved her pliant body to extract every drop of pleasure.

Victoria closed her eyes at the bliss, while knowing she did not need to wait for morning to find out how she was feeling.

She wanted him to stay.

Victoria wanted to hole them up in her bedroom and never leave because it felt as if there were too many obstacles out there.

This love felt as though it might burst from her chest if she let it; it was just too vast to handle.

There were too many feelings that must be kept in check.

For how would he react to her barrage of questions?

Her feelings were in complete disarray.

'You need to go,' Victoria said.

She went to climb off but he did not let her. 'So you can say I got what I came for?'

He felt her short, reluctant laugh as he held her in his arms.

He was starting to know her a little too well and so she lifted her head up and looked at him.

'You do have to go.'

'I can call and tell them that if there's a problem...' And then he hesitated because family came first, especially at times such as this, yet she had edged her way up that list. 'Come back with me.'

It was possibly the most stupid thing to say, but he was still inside her and that allowed a person to say the occasional reckless thing.

'Isn't it a bit early to be meeting the family?' Victoria said, and got off him.

'Exceptional circumstances,' Dominic retorted as he sorted out his clothes. He was annoyed at himself for pushing things, and annoyed at the contrariness of her. 'Victoria, like it or not, we're going to be parents, and trying to sort things out from a distance isn't working out too well, is it?'

'I'm on nights tomorrow,' Victoria said. 'I just want to go to bed and have a long lie-in.'

'So when will I see you?'

'At work, I guess.'

'I meant away from work. I'm not going to have our relationship dictated by how often your ambulance is dispatched to the Castle, and you kicking me out isn't exactly helping us—'

'I'm hardly kicking you out,' Victoria interrupted. 'You have a family that you need to get back to and I need to get some sleep.'

She needed him gone because she was on the edge of telling him she was crazy about him.

On the edge of asking about Lorna and how it had felt to see her again.

If he knew her—the real, insecure her—Victoria was positive that he would not want her any more.

She had never cared about anyone else in the way she cared for him, and it terrified her. She did not want to add a failed relationship between them to the mix.

'You keep asking if there's anything you can do for me,' Victoria said. 'Well, there is. Just stay back.'

'You mean that?' he checked.

'I do.'

She even held the door open for him.

So much for wanting a long sleep, because Victoria was still awake when she heard the first train of the morning clack past.

Dominic, she decided, could be as involved in their baby's life as he chose to be but she would not allow him to get closer to her.

CHAPTER TWELVE

'WHAT TIME DID you get home last night?' Katie Mac-Bride enquired as Dominic came into the kitchen the next morning.

Dominic, who hadn't had to answer that question for two decades, was certainly in no mood to answer it now.

'Did you hear what your mother said?' William prompted. He was sitting at the kitchen table, reading a newspaper. No doubt he had got up at six and gone out to get one, just as he did back home.

'I heard,' Dominic answered. 'I didn't make a note of the time when I got in.'

He had tea and toast all prepared by Katie, and Dominic laughed to himself at his own suggestion last night that Victoria should come here.

Dominic loved his parents very much but they were straight into his business and he could only imagine a very independent Victoria's response to his parents' fussing.

'What time will you be back?' his mother asked as Dominic went to leave at seven when he didn't really need to leave until half past.

'I'm not sure,' Dominic answered. 'And tomorrow I'm on call all weekend so I'll be staying at the hospital.'

'What about Jamie and Lorna?' William asked. 'Will you be in to visit your nephew?'

'I am going to be working!' Dominic pointed out.

'You should speak with your brother instead of avoiding him.'

'Jamie's here now.' Dominic pointed down the hall to the bedroom. 'How can I be avoiding him?'

Except deep down Dominic knew that he was.

Friday night was hell because little William had a run of atrial fibrillation and Dominic had to race Jamie back to be by Lorna's side.

Dominic sat in the waiting room on the cardiac unit and saw on the news that there was an incident at Piccadilly.

He had never felt fear watching the news until he had met Victoria.

It was hell watching flashing lights on the screen and brawls taking place and knowing she may well be in the thick of it.

And what was he supposed to do?

Did he send a text asking if she was okay and just irk her some more?

Or did he just sit there feeling ill while hoping to God she was safe?

She wasn't.

Victoria wasn't gung-ho but she could never be accused of holding back, yet as she climbed out of the vehicle to the sounds of a brawl, for the first time in her career she did hold back.

Victoria did not feel safe.

'Hey!' Glen warned the guy lying on the kerb as he lashed out with his boot. 'We're trying to help.' He looked over to Victoria. 'Can you bring the stretcher closer?' Glen said, and then he asked the police who were holding the man to get a better grip on him.

It was Victoria who drove the patient to hospital while Glen stayed in the back.

Nothing was actually said, but Victoria knew only too well that she wasn't carrying her share of the load.

Glen was lovely; he always was.

He sensed that she had lost her nerve and so he put his big body in between Victoria and the patients during a few of the trickier call-outs. But late on Sunday night, coming into the early hours of Monday morning, after attending a domestic dispute, Glen told her something.

'You need to tell work.'

'I know.'

She was on leave after this shift but she would tell her line manager about the baby this morning, when they returned to base.

And then the wheels would all be put into motion, and on her return from leave her duties would change and Victoria would no longer be operational.

'What time's your ultrasound at?' Glen asked.

'Ten.'

'You'll be wrecked,' he said because they finished at eight.

'I'll grab an hour of sleep at the station after we finish,' Victoria said.

'Is Dominic coming with you?'

'I don't want him to.'

'Let him be there.'

'Just leave it.'

She took a bite of her sandwich. She was not going to be discussing this with Glen, but also, she noted, he didn't offer to come with her this time.

Perhaps now that Glen knew who the father was, he felt that it wasn't his place to offer, but all the same, she felt terribly alone.

Victoria's job was her rock and a huge part of her identity.

She was excited to become a mother, yet it felt a little as if everything familiar was being stripped away.

How *was* she going to work and be a single mum?

Just who would be looking out for the baby on nights such as this?

Would Dominic really be there for them?

She tried to imagine him dropping over to her flat to look after their little one while she headed out, or taking the baby over to his.

How long would that last? How long till he tired of any arrangements they made or, like her father, suddenly got called into work and decided that his job was more important than hers?

Or what if he met someone else, which of course he would one day, and decide that his new family was his priority?

As her mother had done.

And then she tried not to think of the other possibility—the two of them together, knowing the odds were that they wouldn't work. He still hadn't sorted things out with his family. Even with a desperately ill baby the brothers were unable to be close.

And as for her?

Victoria had never been close to anyone.

That was her real fear—that, even with the best of intentions, he might give them a go for the sake of their baby, but that Dominic would one day tire of her and simply leave.

'How do you and Hayley make it work?' Victoria

asked, but she didn't get her answer—a call-out came and as the address was given Victoria recognised it straight away.

'That's Penny.'

They put on the lights and Glen drove skilfully through the dark London streets and soon they were pulling up at her house.

The lights were on both upstairs and down and, as they made their way up the path, Victoria saw that the front door had been left open.

'Through here.' Penny's father was on the phone trying to find out how much longer the ambulance would be, which Victoria knew from experience meant things were bad. She took a breath and went through to the lounge.

'Hello, beautiful!'

Victoria's smile was bright and no one would ever guess that Victoria's heart sank when she saw Penny.

Julia was lying on the sofa with her daughter and holding her little girl's body in her arms.

Penny's hair was loose and it was damp with sweat; her eyes were sunken and she was struggling so hard simply to breathe. Glen put on oxygen as Victoria carefully checked the little girl over.

'I'm going to use the bag to help you breathe, Penny,' Glen said, and as Penny breathed in, Glen assisted her, pushing vital oxygen into her lungs.

She was terribly hot, though as Victoria peeled back the blanket she saw that she still had on her little tutu.

Victoria chatted to the little girl, but made sure she didn't ask too many questions so that Penny could save her energy.

Her lungs were full of fluid and as Victoria inserted an IV into Penny's arm she barely flinched.

'You are such a brave girl,' Victoria said. 'I'm going to give you some medicine now and that's going to get rid of all that horrible fluid that is making it so hard to breathe.'

Penny became a bit agitated but Julia knew why. 'She doesn't like the diuretics because they made her wet herself once, but that doesn't matter, Penny.'

It did to her though.

'I've got a bed pan in the ambulance,' Victoria said, 'and we'll put lots of pads on the stretcher, so if you do have a little accident we'll have you all cleaned up before you go into the Castle.'

Penny nodded and Victoria pushed through the vital medicine.

The oxygen was helping, and with the other medications she started to calm. Soon her breathing was a little deeper, and the horrible mottled tinge to Penny's skin was starting to recede.

They needed to get her to Paddington's.

This time there was no question that she could get onto the stretcher by herself so Glen gently picked Penny up. He placed her on the stretcher and made sure that she was safely secured, and then together he and Victoria raised it up.

'Ready for the off?' Victoria said as she always did.

And always Penny nodded and smiled, or if she wasn't well enough, as was the case today, would do a little thumbs-up sign.

Today though, she spoke. 'Not...' She gasped but she couldn't finish her sentence and Julia moved to reassure her.

'We've got everything with us, Penny,' Julia said, because she always made sure that she had Penny's favourite things.

But Victoria knew that that wasn't what Penny had been trying to say.

Victoria had seen it happen in many patients—they just wanted a moment more in their home, though usually they were much older than Penny when they felt that way.

'It's okay, Penny,' Victoria said. 'We can take a minute.'

Yes, she was time critical, but the priority, too, was to cause the little girl minimum distress, and rushing her out against her wishes would only cause her to get upset. And so she stood and waited as Penny's eyes moved around the room.

And Julia understood then what her daughter had meant when she had tried to say that she wasn't quite ready to leave.

Penny wanted to take a long look at her home.

And she did.

She looked over at the television, which had been paused in the middle of a cartoon, and all of her favourite characters were frozen on the screen. Then her eyes went to the chair and then over to the sofa where she had lain and she was imprinting it all.

Penny didn't know if she would be coming home.

Julia, who was very strong and used to seeing her daughter unwell, was choking up.

'Why don't you get a glass of water, Julia,' Victoria suggested, and as Julia wept in the other room, Penny sat just taking in the memories of her home.

Glen, of course, was tearing up and Penny gave him a stern look that warned him to stop then and there.

Julia bustled back in and saw Penny's eyes linger on a photo. It looked like a holiday snap of the family at the beach. 'Shall we bring that with us, darling?' Julia asked.

Penny nodded and then rested back on the pillows and now she gave her usual little thumbs up.

She was ready.

Peter, her father, gave his daughter a kiss and told her that he was going to lock up and would see her soon at the hospital.

Once in the vehicle they alerted Paddington's to let them know they were on their way along with the details and status of the patient that they were bringing in.

Glen drove and Victoria sat in the back with Julia and Penny. There was no need for sirens as the streets were empty, but the lights were on and if needed Glen would use the siren at traffic lights or if the situation changed.

The mood was sombre.

Usually Julia would read Penny a story on the way to the hospital but she just sat there while the blue lights of the ambulance shadowed her face.

'Story...' Penny said.

'Well, let me see...' Victoria answered. And she let Julia sit quietly and gather herself for whatever lay ahead.

Victoria thought for a moment; she had told Dominic that she didn't believe in fairytales, but growing up she had loved them, just like any little girl.

She had just never had to make one up before.

Victoria thought for a moment and then she told Penny about a turret and a magic castle and a little girl who used to sneak behind the files and find her way up there. And she watched as Penny gave a faint smile so Victoria knew she must be telling the tale okay. 'There's a princess who lives there and she watches over all the babies and children.'

'Truly?' Penny gasped.

'Of course,' Victoria said. 'I told you, it's a magic castle.'

And she held the little girl's hand and told her some more and it really did seem to soothe Penny.

Her colour was terrible though and her heart was galloping, but then Penny looked up at the blacked-out windows and smiled.

Victoria glanced up too and relief flooded her as the familiar roofline came into sight.

The not-so-new Dr Thomas Wolfe was waiting for them. Victoria had been right—he had worked here. She recognised him from many years ago when she had just started to work on the ambulances, but this was no time to reminisce with him.

She was just relieved that someone so skilled was here to greet this very sick little girl.

Thomas listened to the handover as they moved her onto the resuscitation bed. He thanked the paramedics as he examined the patient and Victoria saw his expression was grim as he listened to her back and chest.

'You're doing very well, Penny,' he said to her, and he gently sat her back. She was upright in the bed as she was still struggling to breathe. The nurses worked deftly alongside him, attaching Penny to monitors and leads and pulling up the drugs and IV solutions that Thomas was calling for.

Victoria had done her job—she had delivered Penny safely to the Castle, and that had used to be enough for her. But so badly she wanted to stay and see how Penny was doing.

She actually had to prise herself away.

Maybe it was because she herself was going to be a mother that suddenly things were affecting her more.

Or maybe it was that since Dominic had come into her life she simply felt everything more acutely.

It was as if her emotions had been reset to a heightened level and Victoria felt on the edge of tears as she saw more staff running into the resuscitation room.

'I'm going to go and get a drink,' Glen said.

'Sure.' Victoria nodded and she set about making up the stretcher, telling herself to stop getting so upset, that it was just work.

Of course, Glen didn't really want a drink; his flask was in the ambulance and there was a coffee machine close by.

He walked through the department and stood in the kitchenette; he clung to the bench and told himself to take some deep breaths.

And that was where Dominic found him.

'Hi there,' Dominic said, but he got no response.

He knew that Glen's presence meant that Victoria was here somewhere, but he could see that Glen was struggling, and so, instead of heading out, he spoke with him for a while.

Dominic discovered that indeed Glen and Victoria had been at Piccadilly on Friday.

No, he didn't push for information but he guessed, and rightly so, that the weekend had taken a bit of a toll on both of them. Dominic was very grateful to this man for looking out for her.

And they spoke about the fire at Westbourne Grove and how there had been no choice really but to move forward when they had seen just how precarious Lewis's injuries were.

Then Dominic listened as Glen told him about Penny, about how bad it had been back at the house and how she had asked to stay for one lingering look.

'Poor little mite,' Glen said. 'You just can't help but compare them to your own sometimes.'

And then Glen asked him something.

'Do you remember a child we brought in…?'

And he spoke about a little girl that had been brought in a few months ago, one around the same age as Glen's daughter.

Yes, Dominic remembered it well—it was the same child that Dominic had lost on the operating table.

'I'd do anything for my children,' Glen said, 'and I just hope that for her I did the same, but I wonder if we'd just been a bit quicker extracting her from the vehicle and if we'd—'

'Glen,' Dominic interrupted.

Not unkindly.

He had gone over the very same questions about the same little girl himself, and so had the coroner.

'There was nothing that anyone could have done. Even if she had somehow been operated on at the scene, *still* there was nothing that could have been done.'

'I know that,' Glen admitted. He just needed to hear it again.

And again.

He really did need to talk it through.

'She really got to me.'

'I know,' Dominic said. 'It was awful.'

All losses hit hard, but some had the capacity for major destruction and that was what was happening with Glen.

'Victoria keeps on at me to go and speak to someone about it.'

Dominic was very glad that Victoria was on to things, and he was glad that this partnership looked out for each other.

'I think that would be very wise,' Dominic said. 'And if you do have any more questions, or talking it through raises some, then you can come and talk to me.'

Glen nodded. 'I'm just going to take a minute before I go back out.'

'Sure.'

Dominic walked out through to the department and he saw Victoria standing by the made-up stretcher, reading her phone. Dominic made his way over to her.

She felt him approach but Victoria didn't look up.

'Your colleague is crying in the kitchen,' Dominic told her, and though he kept it light he also let her know what was going on.

'I know.' Victoria looked up then and rolled her eyes. 'I'm going to politely pretend not to notice.'

But she *had* noticed, Dominic knew. Glen had just told him that Victoria had addressed this with him on many an occasion.

'Was it very grim at the house?' he asked.

'Not really,' Victoria said.

And Dominic frowned because Glen had just told him, in detail, that it had been awful—that Penny had asked for a moment to look around before they left and that Julia had become upset.

Then, as casually as anything, she told him that unless she got another call-out this morning, this would be the last time they ran into each other like this.

'I'm probably going to be working in the clinical hub—dispatch—from now on.'

'Is everything okay?'

'It's procedure,' Victoria said. 'I've got two weeks' leave, starting at the end of this shift, but when I come back I shan't be operational.'

'Good,' Dominic said. 'Well, I'll miss seeing you but I think it's better than the risk of being out there.'

'I'll still see you at the Save Paddington's meetings, I hope.' Victoria smiled.

'You shall.'

Dominic was doing his best to stay back and not crowd her.

He was finding it hell.

Maybe he should take her at face value, Dominic reasoned. Maybe he should simply accept it when she said that things did not get to her, and that she really would prefer to go through this alone.

Yet it did not equate to the passionate side she revealed at times and, he was certain, she hurt just as deeply, even if she did not show it.

He should walk away, just treat her as coolly as she said she wanted, but instead he tried another tack.

'I'm expecting a transfer from Riverside,' Dominic said. 'I've actually just been speaking with your father.'

'Lucky you,' Victoria said, and got back to reading her phone.

'What did he say to you, Victoria?' He saw her rapid blink as she deliberately didn't look up. 'When you had that row, what did he say?'

She shook her head. 'I don't want to go over it again.'

'Please do,' Dominic said. 'Of course, if it's too upsetting…'

'It's not that.' She shrugged. 'It just paints me in a rather unflattering light. He pointed out that my mother didn't just leave him.'

She didn't say it verbatim, but he could almost hear Professor Christie saying that she had left her too.

'How does that paint you in an unflattering light?' Dominic asked.

'Well, I can't have been the cutest baby.' She tried to make a joke.

'How old were you when she left?'

'I think it was just before I turned one,' Victoria said with a shrug. 'She didn't even last a year.' And then Victoria pocketed her phone and she looked right at him. 'So you can see why I don't want you flitting in and out of my child's life.' Then she thought about it. 'Not that my mother did. When she decided to leave she left for good.'

'You don't see her at all?'

'No,' Victoria said. 'I found her on social media a couple of years ago. She's got two grown-up sons. I guess they're my half-brothers.'

'Did you make contact?'

'I tried to—they all blocked me.'

'Well, I shan't be doing the same.'

'Not straight away, but you might change your mind and decide to go and live in Scotland, once you've sorted things with your family...'

'Victoria, do you remember when I told you about Lorna and you pointed out that I wasn't your ex?'

She nodded.

'Well, it works both ways—I'm not one of your parents either. I shan't be turning my back on the baby. I shall *always* be there for my child.'

Victoria already knew that.

Deep down, she always had.

After Dominic's initial poor reaction on the night she had told him, he had run after her and had been trying to get *more* involved rather than *less*.

It wasn't the baby she was now trying to protect.

It was herself.

He would be agony to lose and her heart could not take further hurt.

'What about Lorna?' Victoria said, and she silently kicked below the belt. 'Did you say that you'd *always* be there for her too?'

He didn't baulk at her question; Dominic stared her right in the eyes. 'No.'

'I don't believe you.'

'Well, you should, because half Lorna's and my problem was that I'm not very effusive.'

'Did you say you'd always be there for your brother?' Victoria asked, and that kick delivered because this time he flinched.

Not much.

She just saw the slight tightening of his lips and then he righted himself.

'I thought as much.' She shook her head. 'Thanks but no thanks, Dominic. I really do want to do this on my own.'

Dominic looked at Victoria. He was not going to force himself on someone who clearly didn't want him too close in her life.

'Victoria,' Dominic said, 'I will stay back, if that is what helps you. But with one proviso.'

'What's that?'

'If you change your mind, you're to tell me.'

'I shan't be changing my mind,' Victoria said, and then she saw that Glen was making his way towards them. 'I'll see you around.'

CHAPTER THIRTEEN

SEE YOU AROUND!

Dominic had watched her walk out and had resisted yanking her back, but really—*see you around!*

Of course he could not force her to accept his presence at the appointment, nor could he demand anything from her.

He had loathed her working on the ambulance whilst pregnant but at least it had meant that they saw each other regularly.

Now it would just be Save Paddington's meetings and they were always busy. Though there were get-togethers afterwards, there would be no real chance for the two of them to speak.

He could hardly go around to her flat, given how it had ended the last time.

Yet, he could not regret what had taken place.

That night, it had not been just the sex that had soothed. It had been the conversation and just a glimpse of peace on a tumultuous day.

And a glimpse of another side to Victoria.

He was waiting for the transfer from Riverside to arrive but that could well be hours away. Still, rather than head off and get some rest, he hung around in case

Victoria came back in, knowing that it might be their last chance to speak.

The nurses were stretched thin.

Karen was working in the resuscitation area and watching Penny while also trying to take some observations on a wriggling two-year-old. When the buzzer went over Penny's bay, Dominic stood to answer it and Karen gave a nod of thanks to him.

'Hello.'

He smiled down to Penny.

'You're not a nurse,' Penny said. She was looking a bit better and could speak in short sentences, but even that seemed to deplete her.

'No,' he said. 'I'm not, but Karen is just giving a baby some medicine and doing its obs. Can I help you with anything?'

'I want some ice.'

'I think I can manage that.'

He went and filled a cup from the dispenser and then began feeding Penny a spoon of ice chips.

'Mum's speaking to the doctor,' Penny said.

'She shouldn't be too long,' Dominic reassured. 'How are you feeling now?'

'Better.'

'That's good.'

She was a little anxious and he guessed that tonight she must have had a fright, so he did not place the cup down but instead let her get her breath for a moment and waited until she spoke again.

'A princess lives in the tower,' Penny said, pointing to the roof. 'Victoria told me.'

'That's good to know.' He smiled because it would seem that even if Victoria didn't believe in fairytales she knew how to tell them. There were so many sides to Victoria.

And he wanted to know them all.

'A beautiful princess,' Penny added, and he waited for her to take a couple of breaths before she continued. 'She watches over all the children.'

'What about the handsome prince?' Dominic asked.

'Victoria didn't mention him.'

Of course she didn't! Dominic thought as he smiled.

He fed her a few more chips of ice. He guessed that, more than ice, Penny wanted some company and so he chatted about magic and fairies and wishes that came true and, because of his accent, she asked about the Loch Ness monster and if he believed it.

'Who, Nessie?' He made it sound as if the monster was a close friend. 'My brother and I saw her one holiday many years ago.' And because he was so serious it made it more believable somehow, so Penny lay there and smiled and told him one of her wishes.

'I wish I could have ballet lessons.'

'Well, I'm sure the princess is working on that as we speak,' Dominic said, and then turned as Julia came in.

'Oh, thank you, Doctor,' she said.

'No problem.'

'What did the doctor say?' Penny asked her mother.

'That they're going to keep you here for a few days. It's her second home…' Julia added to Dominic, taking the cup of ice chips and smiling as she did so.

He could see that Julia had put on some make-up and was doing everything in her power to hide her own terrified heart.

Children often amazed him, Dominic thought, but then adults did too.

Julia had just been delivered terrible news about Penny, Dominic knew.

This wasn't going to be just a couple of nights' stay.

He had heard Thomas speaking with Karen and the news wasn't good.

A viral infection was ravaging Penny's already damaged heart and had pushed her into a dangerous level of heart failure.

'Where's Dad?' Penny asked her mum.

'He's moving the car or he'll get clamped again!' Julia said, and then she turned it into a funny story, reminding Penny how Dad's car had got clamped a couple of times.

And either the guy was out there weeping, Dominic thought, or he really was trying to sort out a car that had been haphazardly parked in the race to get to his desperately sick child.

Julia chatted and fussed, and then in came Peter smiling and waving at Penny; he came over and gave his little girl a kiss.

And Dominic watched.

You wouldn't know that they were in agony.

Unless you knew.

And suddenly Dominic did.

Victoria was hurting.

Of course she was.

And probably she hurt a bit more with each and every passing day.

He thought of Glen, idly chatting, saying how you would do anything for your children.

And the firefighters who had run into a building to save children that weren't even theirs.

Every single day it must be rammed home to her just what her mother had done.

* * *

Victoria *was* hurting.

She and Glen sat in the vehicle and Victoria got out her flask so they could have a coffee as the sun was coming up over London.

'I'm going to miss this,' Victoria said.

'You'll be back.' Glen smiled.

'I shall be,' Victoria agreed. 'But even though I'll miss not being on the road, I am ready to give it away for a while.'

Since she had found out that she was going to be a mother, she knew it wasn't just her life she was risking at times.

It wasn't the heavy lifting, more the unpredictability of some patients, which meant that once she told work that she was pregnant, Victoria would probably be moved into dispatch.

Glen had looked out for her these couple of weeks and it was time now for her to look out for him.

Of course she wasn't going to politely ignore his tears; it had just been something she'd said to Dominic.

They looked out for each other and she didn't want to leave without knowing he was taking care of himself.

'Glen,' Victoria said, 'did you see about speaking to someone?'

He nodded. 'I've got an appointment in the morning. That's why I didn't offer to take you to the ultrasound.'

'Have you told Hayley?'

'Yep,' he said. 'She's relieved,' Glen told her. 'It's our anniversary now and she said it's the best present I could give her.'

'You've got that nice wine too,' Victoria reminded him.

'And a ring.'

'How *do* you make it work?' Victoria asked him again, and this time the radio didn't go off so he thought for a moment and then answered.

'You stop being too proud for your own good.'

She guessed he was referring to a recent conversation with Hayley, and that he had finally heeded the advice and was getting himself some help.

'So we're both getting ourselves sorted after this shift,' Victoria said.

'Starting to,' Glen corrected. 'Let him be there for the ultrasound, Victoria. Whatever happens between the two of you, whether you're a couple or not, you can parent together, surely?'

Could they? Victoria pondered.

Who was she to deny her child a wonderful parent?

It would have made all the difference to her.

CHAPTER FOURTEEN

THE TRANSFER FINALLY arrived and required surgery.

Dominic liked the quiet of theatre.

Some surgeons chatted or listened to music; Dominic liked quiet so he could concentrate, especially when he had been on call all weekend.

By seven in the morning his latest patient was settled on the ward. After he had done a ward round and checked on all his other patients and handed them over, Dominic was tired enough to want to go home.

But instead Dominic showered and then hung around.

He knew that Victoria's ultrasound was at ten.

But he wasn't just there for that reason; there was another thing that he needed to do.

Victoria was right to be cautious about getting involved with him.

She didn't need a man who came with baggage. He had been determined to get things sorted with his family before he approached Victoria. But then the baby had been sprung upon him and things had gone wayward for a while.

Dominic knew that the problems within his family needed to be dealt with, but more importantly, he finally felt ready.

He went to his locker and then Dominic walked through the hospital and made his way to the cardiac unit.

Some days were hard, when you were least expecting them to be.

Other days were unexpectedly not.

He walked onto the cardiac unit and there was Penny, hooked up to monitors and IVs but looking peaceful. She smiled and gave him a little wave.

Dominic waved back and then he went up to the nurses' station where Thomas stood.

'Morning,' he said.

'Good morning.' Thomas nodded.

Dominic was waiting for a nurse so he could explain that he was just here to visit, but for the moment they were all tied up so he stood at the desk.

Thomas didn't exactly invite conversation and he was back to busily writing up some notes.

'Hi, Rebecca,' Dominic said as she approached.

'Dr Scott,' Thomas greeted, and Dominic frowned at the rather formal address of her.

'Dr Wolfe,' Rebecca said, and her voice sounded strained but she pushed out her lovely smile for Dominic. 'What are you doing on the cardiac unit?' she asked him.

'My nephew's a patient here—William MacBride.'

'Oh,' Rebecca said in surprise. 'I thought the name was familiar. I'm actually here to see him.'

'I'll come back later, then,' Dominic offered. He didn't understand the tension between these two but he didn't want to make things worse. But then Rebecca declined his offer to leave.

'No, no, I need to speak with Dr Wolfe first and I have another couple of patients to see. Go ahead.'

A nurse came over then—it was Rosie—and Dominic explained why he was here and she waved him on.

Really, he could have just popped in, but he had wanted the separation, for this was not a doctor visiting.

It was a brother, a brother-in-law and an uncle that had come to visit this morning.

He looked through the glass as he approached and saw the little family.

Lorna was holding William, who was attached to monitors, but he looked rested and pink in his mother's arms.

And there was Jamie hovering over them.

Dominic could have waited until his parents arrived to drop in on them, but he had never needed the shield of his parents. He had just needed the ability to look his brother and Lorna in the eye.

Without hurt or malice.

'Hey.'

He knocked on the open door and Lorna looked up and he could see that she was startled.

Jamie stood up a touch straighter and was clearly nervous at Dominic's unexpected arrival.

'How is he doing?' Dominic asked.

'Better,' Jamie said. 'They've got him on something called beta...' He struggled with all the new terminology.

'Beta-blockers.' Dominic nodded. 'They slow the heart down and steady things.'

'I think I might need some,' Lorna said, and let out a nervous laugh as she made a feeble joke.

Oh, it seemed such a long time ago since they had been together and so much had happened since then.

'Well, you've had a very difficult time with William.'

Dominic chose his words carefully, refusing to allude to the situation between the three of them.

It was over with.

He gave her a smile and saw that she relaxed.

'I got this for William,' Dominic said, and handed over the wrapped present to Lorna.

She opened it while holding William, and with all his drips and things it took a while, but when Lorna saw what it was she smiled. It was a little Scottie dog, wearing a tartan bow.

'He's gorgeous,' she said. 'We didn't think to bring any toys with us. It will be nice to have something for his cot here.'

'Here,' Dominic said, and handed Jamie the card. Knowing how useless Jamie was with money Dominic had put in a generous cheque. It wasn't for the baby though. 'I thought you could get something for the nursery or a pusher or whatever.'

'Thank you.'

But it was the words on the card that mattered the most to Jamie and he read them again.

Dear Lorna and Jamie,
Congratulations on the birth of William.
   I am thrilled to be an uncle and looking for-
ward to watching him grow up. I know you'll be
amazing parents.
Love, Dominic

And Jamie knew that his brother always meant every word.

'Do you want a hold of him?' Jamie asked, and his voice was a bit choked. 'Or maybe...' He hesitated, worried that it might be too much for his brother, but Dominic *had* meant every word.

He was ready now to be in his nephew's life.

'I'd love to hold him.'

Dominic held many babies in a day's work but he hadn't held a baby outside of that parameter, ever.

And it was very different.

William really was a gorgeous baby and had the MacBride chin and long, long hands and feet. The change of arms woke him and he opened up his eyes and gave his uncle a smile.

'You don't remember me from last week, do you?' Dominic said to him. 'Because I was sticking needles in you then.'

'He's looking better though?' Lorna anxiously asked.

'He is. And I know you must be terrified but we're a tough lot and I'm sure that he's going to be fine.' Dominic held him for a couple of moments and, as he did, it occurred to him that in the not too distant future he would be holding a baby of his own.

How could you ever walk away from your own child?

Dominic wasn't one to let his emotions run away with him, but as he looked at the little baby, he felt a choke of emotion on behalf of Victoria.

He made a choice then to be patient, a choice that he would wait for however long it took for her to trust in him.

Not just as a father.

He had far greater plans for them than that.

Dominic handed the baby back to his mother and then he shook his brother's hand.

'Congratulations,' Dominic said, and he could finally look him in the eye and smile.

'Oh!'

He turned at the sound of his mother's voice and saw the concern in his father's expression.

'I was just dropping in to see how William was doing,' Dominic explained.

'Is everything okay?' William Senior asked as he came in.

'All's good,' Dominic said. 'I'll see you back at home. And, Lorna,' he added. 'If you want a *proper dinner* or to stay at my home, then you're very welcome.' He turned to his mother. 'But I've been working all night, remember, so can you please keep it down.'

And they were back to being a family.

Dominic made his way back to Accident and Emergency. He had a coffee and killed time, watching as a nurse rolled her eyes as she did her best to hold on to her temper as she spoke with someone on the phone.

'I am sorry about that but I wasn't working last night. I'll try and find out for you.' She pressed Mute and let out a hiss. 'That man!'

'Who?'

'Professor Christie over at Riverside.'

'What does he want?'

'A transfer last night...' She shook her head. 'Don't worry, I know you're not on.'

'It's fine.'

He picked up the phone and on the other end of the line he heard the great Professor Christie berate a member of staff.

'Hello,' Dominic said. 'Dominic MacBride speaking.'

'Oh!' Professor Christie said, and he switched to charming. 'Sorry about that, I'm working with clumsy imbeciles this morning.'

He had thought about it for a long time and examined it from many angles and, in this instance, Dominic *did* know what to say.

'Well—' Dominic's voice was curt '—that might have something to do with the fact that they're working alongside an arrogant git. So,' he asked, and adopted a more professional tone, 'how can I help you?'

He saw the nurse turn with eyes wide as he heard the professor splutter into the phone.

'*What* did you just say?' Professor Christie demanded.

'Do you want me to repeat it?' Dominic calmly replied. 'Or would you like me to come over now and say it to your face?'

'Now, listen here—'

'I do listen,' Dominic said. 'I listen very carefully and I also think before I speak.'

His voice held a warning and there was silence on the other end of the line.

'Now,' Dominic said, 'what did you want to know about the patient?'

CHAPTER FIFTEEN

VICTORIA SAT IN the waiting room of the Imaging Department.

There was a television up high on the wall but Victoria was too busy replying to some emails about the next Save Paddington's meeting to watch it.

Then her phone rang and Victoria grimaced when she saw that it was her father who was calling her.

He rarely called. In fact, it was always Victoria who called him.

Perhaps there had been a change of heart, Victoria thought.

'Hi, Dad,' she said.

'Who's the father of the baby?'

'Why?' Victoria asked.

'Just tell me.'

Victoria sat there.

Her father had shown absolutely no interest in this baby and from his very brusque tone she didn't think he sounded particularly interested now.

In fact, he sounded furious as he spoke on. 'You said that he was in Scotland…'

'Why do you want to know?'

'Well, I've just had some upstart insult me. Dominic MacBride…'

Her heart was bumping against the wall of her chest. 'What did he say?'

She closed her eyes as her father repeated it.

What the hell was Dominic thinking to speak to her father like that? Dominic, who insisted his responses were measured, clearly hadn't thought this one through.

For it made a future impossible.

Any get-togethers would be fraught and tense.

And in that moment she felt as if she were about to cry, for she was mentally waving goodbye to Christmases and Easters and family celebrations and she had been trying so hard not to think of them.

'Well?' Professor Christie demanded. 'Is he the father?'

'Yes,' Victoria answered. She was cross with Dominic, even if she privately agreed with what had been said, but she did not tell her father that. Instead she told him a truth. 'And I'm very glad that he is.'

Dominic would be a wonderful father, she absolutely knew.

She was glimpsing Christmases and birthdays again, and even if she might not be in the picture, her baby would be taken care of during celebrations whenever it was in his care.

He deserved to be here.

She simply ended the call because there was another major incident occurring, but this time it was with her heart.

It wasn't just that he deserved to be there.

He would be the one she would call on if anything was wrong.

It would be Dominic's voice she would need if their baby was ill, or hot, or fussing.

Glen seemed to think it was possible but she didn't

know how to let him into the baby's life without revealing how she really felt.

Yet, he did deserve to be there.

And so, before she could talk herself out of it she sent a hurried text.

Can you come to the ultrasound?

She hit Send and then panicked because that sounded too needy, and then started to write another.

You can come to the ultrasound if you still want to.

But that didn't read right and so she didn't hit Send but then she thought of him waking to the first, as he was probably asleep and would read it and think there was something wrong.

What if there was something wrong?

She needed him here.

And then suddenly he was there.

She knew, as she always did, whenever Dominic was close. He stood over her as she stared down at her phone and then she looked up. 'You got here fast.'

'I thought I'd hang around in case you changed your mind,' Dominic said as he took a seat by her side.

He would not rush in and scare her with his feelings. That text, asking him to be here, was enough for now.

'Have you been speaking to my father?' she accused.

'Aye.'

'What did you say?' she asked, wondering if he would be vague but Dominic told her exactly.

'He was talking down to a member of his staff and one of ours. I just said he was an arrogant git. That's all.'

'So how is it going to be when you see him?' She

would not admit to the family get-togethers that she dreamed might happen one day. 'At the hospital and things.'

'I'll be civil.' He looked over to her angered face. 'Victoria, do you really think there are going to be many cosy get-togethers with me, him and the baby?'

'No,' she said, and she was struggling to keep her feelings in, because what he had said didn't bode well for any chance for them.

'But if they do happen,' Dominic said, 'then I will play the part and do the right thing, but he has to know that I know what he's like. I will not let him inflict his bloody nature on my child nor on the mother of my child. I just served him a warning today.'

His lips were taut and his words were clipped and Victoria nodded because deep down she knew that he was right.

It wasn't fear of confrontation that flooded her now; it was a wash of relief that came over her, though she tried not to show it. Finally there was someone in her corner where there never had been before, and even if he was there just to guard their child she was very glad that Dominic was on board.

'Are you nervous?' he asked.

'Are you?'

'Yes.'

And they smiled because given what had happened to Dominic, and given their short history, perhaps he should be, but Dominic nudged her and they looked up at the television.

'Look.'

It was that image of them from Westbourne Grove.

It seemed like ages ago, but it had been just a couple of weeks.

Yet so much had changed.

Images of the protestors outside the hospital came onto the screen.

The fire had been a terrible day.

It had changed so many lives, and the fight to save some of them was ongoing. Children were still desperately ill, and yet, from such a terrible event good had prevailed.

Angela Marton was now talking about the fight to save Paddington Children's Hospital and saying that Londoners did not want to lose the institution that brought hope to so many.

'I want my baby to be born here,' Victoria said.

'Our baby,' he corrected.

'So you believe me now,' she nudged.

'Victoria, the more I know you, the more I'm amazed at the speed with which you dropped your knickers.'

'Stop it!'

'It's true. That condom had probably expired.'

'So why are you nervous, then?'

'Because, like every other parent, I want our baby to be fine.' He gave her a smile. 'You do believe in fairytales.'

'I don't.'

'Penny told me about the princess.'

'How is Penny?'

'Don't worry about that now.'

'I'm not worried,' she lied. 'Just tell me.'

'She's got a virus and she's in severe heart failure.'

She thought of Penny's beautiful eyes taking in the lounge and she prayed, so hard, that she would one day be back there.

'Do you think she'll be okay?'

'I don't know, Victoria. She's got a long road ahead of her.'

'Victoria Christie.'

She stood up for the radiographer when her name was called.

'Come through.'

She was shown to a little cubicle and asked to put on a gown.

'Then go in and lie down, and I'll be through shortly,' she said.

Victoria changed and went through to the little room and got up on the examination couch, putting a blanket over her legs.

And Dominic sat by her side.

The radiographer came in then and they chatted about dates and confirmed, when she had a feel of Victoria's stomach, that indeed she did have a full bladder.

They had a little laugh, then the radiographer's pager went off and she said that she'd be back soon.

They were both very quiet.

Dominic was probably feeling sick, Victoria thought, given what had happened the last time he was in this situation.

Dominic did not feel sick.

Not in the least.

He would not be demanding a DNA test.

He knew for a fact this baby was his.

Victoria didn't *need* anyone.

Except maybe she did.

'I'm nervous.' She just came out and said it. 'What if there's something wrong?'

'Then we shall deal with it together.'

He held her hand.

Oh, she did need a handhold because it felt like silk wrapping around not just her fingers but her heart.

She started to cry.

'It will be okay,' Dominic said, and he peeled off some tissues.

'I'm just tired,' she said. 'It was a busy shift and I'm worried about Penny.'

'I know,' he said.

But it wasn't just that.

'I'm sorry I was terse with your father.'

'It's not that.'

She was glad of it now.

It was her mother.

'I love this baby so much already. I don't get how she could just leave me like that.'

'Nor do I,' he told her. 'Victoria, I shan't be doing the same.'

And Glen was right; whatever happened between them, they would do what was best for the baby.

But it wasn't just that.

It was a huge comfort to know her baby would have such a wonderful father, yet the fears about Dominic were not for her child now. They were for her own heart.

The radiographer came in and he peeled off more tissues and she pressed them onto her eyes.

'I'm enthusiastic to see our baby,' Dominic said, and that made her smile. He hadn't rushed in and said it when her eyes had pleaded for him to in the canteen.

He said it now when he meant it.

'So am I.'

And there it was.

All that fuss for something so small.

Yet so beautiful and so vital and alive.

And they weren't really listening to dates and looking at crown rump length and things.

Just watching the baby with its tiny arms and legs and even fingers and toes. It was just a moment they shared.

He looked from the screen to Victoria, and there was the flash of fresh tears in her eyes. He would never leave her, yet she didn't even know. He didn't care if it took for ever; he would get right into that guarded heart. What had happened when their baby had been made was a rare magic; he bent over and gave her a light kiss. This man could not hold back any longer!

'I love you.'

He had sworn not to push her, but he couldn't not say it. He did not want her to go another moment in this life without love.

Though because he was all stoic and Scottish, and there was someone else in the room, that was all the romance she was going to get.

It meant everything and more to hear that, but she was certain it was just the emotion of the moment. The dates matched exactly and maybe Dominic had just gotten a bit carried away.

She lay there as his hand remained over hers but those fears in her head beat faster than the heart on the screen.

It was like the world was all in this room—his hand, their baby—and she was scared for the lights to go on, for she would surely wake up alone.

And then it was over.

The images would be looked at, they were told, but everything seemed perfect, and Victoria could now get dressed.

'Thank you,' Victoria said, but she was almost scared to move because the tears were threatening.

'I'll wait in Reception,' Dominic said, but as he turned to go she started to cry.

'What are you crying over?' he asked. 'Your mum?'

It would be so easy to nod and say yes and perhaps a whole lot safer too, because she was scared to reveal herself.

Then she thought about something else that Glen had said, about not being too proud for your own good and so *this* woman met his eyes in the ultrasound room and made her confession and told him her truth.

'You,' Victoria said. 'I'm crying over you.'

'Cry *on* me, then.'

He pulled her into his arms and held her as she wept, and she told him her fears; she had so many and he dealt with each in turn.

'You might change your mind.'

'Never.' Dominic knew that he would never change his mind.

And he sounded so sure, and here in his arms she was brave enough to voice her fears for them.

'You loved Lorna.'

'Not like this,' Dominic told her. 'I've never loved like this.'

She could hear the steady beat of his heart while hers was racing, and she could feel his quiet strength.

It wasn't the first time she had cried but it was the first time she had cried in someone's arms and so she voiced her deepest fear.

'If there wasn't the baby…'

'Then you'd still be here in my arms.'

And his deep voice was soft and it felt like the truth but she disputed it all the same. 'You stayed back.'

'You asked me to.'

'But before you knew about the baby you didn't make a move.'

'Neither did you,' he pointed out.

'I stayed back because I don't know how to make things work between us,' Victoria said.

'And I stayed back because I do.'

She frowned into his chest.

'Victoria, I told you at the start I was in the middle of something; I wasn't going to land it all on us and come into a relationship jaded and bitter. I needed to sort things out properly.'

She thought about that for a moment and then he spoke some more.

'Now I have sorted it out. I've taken the baby a present, I've had a hold and I've told Lorna she's very welcome in my home.'

'Do you still love her?' Victoria asked. 'You can't undo love.'

'Believe me, you can unravel it,' Dominic said. 'It pretty much came undone the day I found out. Victoria, I haven't been steering clear of Lorna because I have feelings for her. Not positive ones anyway. The last months have been hell, more over my family and brother, but I'll tell you this, since that night, I've thought about *you* every day.'

'Every day?'

'Every minute of every day.'

She looked up to him and she knew he was telling the truth. And that was what had been missing for ever, being thought of by another, every minute of every day.

She thought of her father and his money and occasional gifts.

And her mother who had simply walked away.

But she didn't just think about the bad things. Instead there were thoughts of Glen and how he carried his family in his heart throughout his working day.

And she was starting to believe that Dominic did the same.

'Go and get dressed,' Dominic told her, and he helped her from the examination couch. 'You need to get some sleep and so do I.'

And so she went to the ladies'.

Victoria was practical like that.

And got dressed.

Then she headed out to Reception where he was waiting and he gave her a smile as if he hadn't just rocked her world.

They took the scenic route and as they walked through the quadrangle it was as if the oxygen ratio in the air that she breathed was altered, a bit higher, the colours brighter, the air kinder.

'Thank you for being there today,' Victoria said as they came out to the ambulance foyer and she paused to say goodbye.

'Didn't you hear a word of what I said back in there?' Dominic lightly teased. 'Do you really think I'm going to let you disappear into the underground again? You're to come home with me and I'm not taking no for an answer this time.'

'What's wrong with mine?'

'I want you in my bed.'

CHAPTER SIXTEEN

AND VICTORIA WANTED to be in his bed too.

'I'm very tired,' she warned with a smile as they drove away from Paddington's.

'Victoria,' he said, 'I've been on call all weekend and you look like hell.'

She looked at him all unshaven and with dark circles under his eyes. 'So do you.'

'Good,' Dominic said, and glanced over to her, 'so you'll be able to keep your hands off me, then.'

God, but he turned her on.

His home was a large apartment, close to the hospital. They took the stairs up to his floor and, as he let them in, there were all the signs of a family in residence. Victoria was very used to coming home to her flat alone and finding it exactly as she had left it, but Dominic read a note that had been left on a table in the hall.

'I just saw them back at the hospital,' Dominic told her. 'But it says that they won't be back till this evening.'

She was too tired to look around but there was a nice feel to the place and, as she glanced in the living room, she saw two heavy-looking leather sofas with rugs over the back of them.

A stint of nights, then hanging around for the ultrasound and all the emotion of before, had left Victoria so tired that she felt cold despite the warm day.

They stepped into his bedroom and she looked at the large bed and wanted to sink into it.

'I am so going to enjoy sleeping with you,' Dominic said as he closed the drapes and turned on a bedside light, and she laughed.

'And I am so going to enjoy sleeping with you.'

She slipped off her clothes and got into bed. It had the wonderful, soapy, fragrant scent of him that was now familiar. Victoria suddenly realised that she had never seen him naked. But she was about to get that pleasure now, and she couldn't wait.

Dominic took off his shirt. She saw his pale skin and the dark hair of his chest and she just lazily watched. He undid his belt and as he undressed she saw strong thighs and then his tumescent male beauty.

'We *are* going to sleep,' he promised, yet Victoria wasn't so sure because she was starting to change her mind. There are moments so special that they have to be marked in some way, and this was one of them. So she stretched and sighed as he climbed into bed and turned off the light, and they lay there as a siren went past.

'Thank God it's not you out there,' Dominic said, and he pulled her closer into him. 'Every time I hear a siren I think of you, even before I found out that you were pregnant. I've been so worried about you out there.'

'I will be again,' she warned, because her career was incredibly important to her and she definitely would be going back.

'I know that you will,' Dominic said, 'but you shan't ever be out there again without knowing that I love you.'

And then she looked at Dominic and saw right down

to his soul, and found out that she resided there and that she had ever since their first kiss.

She lifted her face towards him and he kissed not, at first, her mouth but her cheeks and eyes and then he kissed her lips long and slow.

A goodnight kiss, even though it was morning.

The kind of *I'm not going anywhere* kiss that she had never known, and then he held her tight in his arms as they drifted off to sleep together.

For the first time they lay together to the sounds floating up from the street and the bliss of being in each other's arms. They needed no more than this right now.

It was a sleep like no other.

The end of nights and their first together ensured that it was the sweetest, deepest sleep for them both.

Victoria rolled onto her side and he wrapped around her and peace was made.

It was Victoria who stirred first. Dominic was curved into her and she was disorientated as to place and time, for the room was dark and the direction she faced unfamiliar, but she was blissfully certain of the man in whose arms she lay.

Who knows how we awaken together? she thought.

That moment when you realise someone else is present and by your side.

When respite has been taken and you awake peaceful, and there is no need for a frantic examination for you to know it is a better world.

And it was.

His hand was on her stomach and she lay with eyes open to the darkened room, half asleep, half awake and completely content. Then Victoria closed her eyes as his hand roamed the curve of her hip and he moved in closer.

Dominic kissed her bare shoulder and his hand toyed with her breast. She felt the pinch of his finger and thumb on her nipple and the nudge of him between her legs. She turned her face to him and they shared a kiss that was slow, but then both wanted more and so she rolled in his arms for just that. As she did so Dominic moved too. He held himself over her and halted her on her back, resting his elbows by her head and pushing up on his arms. She had never felt so deliciously trapped, yet so safe in love.

On so many occasions Victoria had looked down when he silently demanded that her eyes meet his, but now she looked up to his gaze. Her hand came to the back of his head and she levered herself up to meet his mouth. But it was his kiss this time and so he pressed her back into the pillows and claimed her mouth as below she parted her legs for him.

The feel of him inside her made her shiver, though their bodies were warm and still loose from sleep. His kiss was deep and intense and they moved slowly at first, revelling in the feel of togetherness and the naked heat of their skin. They simply entwined into one as they forgot they were parents-to-be and found out the couple they had now become.

Each measured thrust he delivered brought her a little more undone.

And she was his.

For all the declarations Dominic had offered, when she had given none, with each building sob that she tried to hold in, she revealed herself to him some more.

He placed his hands on the bed, either side of her breasts, and he moved up onto outstretched arms. The separation between them allowed her to lean up on the pillows as he took her, in short rapid thrusts, as she clasped his face and took his lips in a deep kiss.

It was shockingly intimate for both of them—the kissing, the feeling, the watching each other so close to the edge.

Then she closed her eyes, not to him but because the feelings were intense. He moved faster despite the slow caress of his tongue and she searched for a headboard to cling to but settled instead for his solid arms. She couldn't resist the urge to tilt her hips and take him in more deeply.

Everything gathered tight within and Victoria wanted to twist or to lift her knees, almost to shield herself from the throes of frenzy, but instead her hands moved up his arms and her fingertips pressed into his shoulders and she came hard.

And there was nowhere for her heart to hide any more.

Dominic sunk down from his arms and she accepted the weight like a raft, and for a moment they lay breathless.

She waited, but this time regret did not arrive.

'Are you going to say you've made a mistake again?' Dominic asked in that familiar wry tone.

'Well, if it is a mistake, then I intend to keep on repeating it.'

She rolled to her side and they lay staring at each other for a while.

And the feeling remained.

So she told him something she never had said to anyone. 'I love you.'

'Good.'

'And I'm sorry that I asked about Lorna.'

'Don't be, the air needed to be cleared there. We're all going to be in each other's lives. But know this—I've never felt the way I do about you with anyone else. And I tell you now, I know he wouldn't but if my brother touched a hair on your head I would kill him.'

She smiled, because it would never happen, and his voice made her shiver with delight.

'You don't fight,' Victoria pointed out.

'My love for you is savage,' he said, and as he looked at Victoria he decided that she deserved a savage kind of love.

He made her entire skin tingle, just with the stroke of his finger on her arm.

She looked deep into his eyes, and yes, he could be crabby at times, but she liked that. She liked that he did not fight and that the man she loved could never hurt another. Even when they had fought over Penny that day, he had still put the patient first.

She liked his strength and how he fought, not with fists but by holding on to what was right.

'You've been sleeping on my side,' Dominic said, and she smiled, because he made her believe in fairy-tales after all. 'I mean it,' he said, and he knelt up and leant over her. First he turned on the bedside light and then he opened a drawer.

From there he took out a little, dark, velvet box and offered her a warning. 'This isn't a ring.'

'I would hope not, given that we've only had one date.'

'Victoria,' he said in that gorgeous brogue that had her toes curl beneath the sheets. 'We are going to have many, many more. You'll be getting a ring but, for now, I want you to have these. I really have been thinking of you all the time and I hope that these will show you how much.'

He opened the box as Victoria sat up in the bed and when she looked she saw a pair of beautiful earrings. Her heart squeezed and her fingers wanted to touch them but for now she simply looked at a gift from the heart.

'They're Scottish pearls,' he told her. 'I'm lousy at one-night stands and I wanted to get you something. When I was in Scotland I saw these and while I was talking to the jeweller I found out quite a bit about them—pearls are complex things,' Dominic said. 'The oyster tries to protect itself from intruders, and from that something very beautiful is formed.'

They were golden hued and the most beautiful pearls that she had ever seen, but more than that it was the care and thought with which they had been chosen that meant so much to her.

Yes, diamonds might be for ever, but they didn't count unless they were given with love.

Those long fingers were nimble and he carefully put them in for her and, as he did, he asked her a question. 'Do you know what daunts me when I think about a future with you?'

Victoria could think of many things that might.

An unplanned pregnancy from a one-night stand, her job, her independence, to name a few, but then he broke in.

'Nothing daunts me,' Dominic said. 'I had sworn off relationships until I met you. I know we agreed to no more than what happened that night but I was always going to ask you out. I made up my mind in Scotland. I decided that once I had properly sorted things out with my family I would see if we could give things a try. If you said no, then these earrings were still for you, because what happened between us was amazing. I never thought I could trust anyone again, but I do. And the thought of a future with you thrills me.'

She put her fingers to her ears and felt the gorgeous pearls, and then she looked over to Dominic.

This beautiful, rugged man had offered her his heart and she had never been this close to anyone before.

And what he had said applied both ways, for as she looked to a future with Dominic, there was nothing that daunted.

Yes, it thrilled her, in fact.

And then as they kissed, as they lay with the world at their feet, they heard a noise. Victoria, on hearing the front door opening, pulled away and grimaced.

The day had run away from them and there were voices from the hallway. This was so not how she wanted to meet his family.

'They won't come in,' he said.

'And I can't go out.' Victoria groaned, having visions of herself being trapped hiding in his room all night.

'Why ever not?' he asked.

'What will they think?' Victoria asked, aghast at the prospect. 'I can hardly just walk out of your bedroom and meet the family.'

'Well, if you were the type for a one-night stand with a man you barely knew, then I get that it might be awkward…'

He made her laugh and she knew then that they would tease each other about their torrid tryst for ever.

He made everything fine.

Better than fine.

'I'll tell them that I've been seeing you for months,' Dominic suggested, 'which I have been.'

It was no lie. They had noticed each other right from the day they had met.

It was actually now bliss to lie in bed with him and to hear the sounds of his family outside.

'Lorna's here.' It was Dominic who grimaced a bit when he heard her voice, because though he had meant it when he had said that she could come for dinner or stay here, he knew it might be a bit much for Victoria to deal with so soon. 'Do you have a problem with that?'

'None.' Victoria grinned; after all, she was in his bed. But then she thought about it more seriously for a moment and the answer was still the same, so she shook her head. 'None.'

'Good,' Dominic said, and he rolled out of bed and started to pull on some clothes. 'Though we might keep it to ourselves about the baby for now.'

'I know that it must all feel a bit rushed,' Victoria said, thinking of how he had said he felt when he found out that Lorna was pregnant.

'Hardly rushed,' he said. 'I'm thirty-eight.'

Dominic was pulling on his jeans and she would remember that moment for ever. The moment she knew, completely, that they were meant to be.

And then he looked over and smiled as he realised the difference in his feelings between now and the last time that he had thought he was about to become a father. Still there was no need to dwell for they had moved past all that now. 'I'm just warning you,' he said, 'that when they find out they'll make an awful fuss.'

'I can't wait for the fuss,' Victoria said, and she thought of grandparents who would be thrilled at the news, and uncles and aunts and cousins and feuding brothers who had sorted things out. 'As soon as William is more stable we'll share the good news.'

She couldn't wait to get out there, but was actually quite nervous when they finally did.

The MacBrides were all in the kitchen. Jamie and Lorna and Dominic's father were sitting at the table, and his mother, a very small woman, was at the oven.

'Well, hello,' his mother said when together they walked in, and she looked a bit taken back when she saw that Dominic had company.

'This is Victoria,' Dominic introduced. 'She's been on nights too.'

'You never said that you were seeing anyone!' his mother scolded, though she smiled to Victoria.

'Well, we haven't exactly been speaking,' Dominic reminded her. 'But Victoria is very much in my life. Victoria, this is my mother, Katie.'

She met William and Katie, and Jamie and Lorna, who she had, of course, already met, but it was different this time because she was being introduced and integrated into all the main threads of this beautiful man's life.

'How is William doing now?' Victoria asked Lorna, and felt very glad that she had been up-front about knowing Dominic when they were at the hotel.

'He's doing well. Rebecca, the surgeon, doesn't seem to think surgery is necessary at this stage.'

As easily as that they chatted and Victoria understood what Dominic had meant about needing to be properly free from baggage, for there were no dark feelings harboured, no grudges and absolutely no jealousy at all.

'He's getting excellent care,' Jamie said, and then looked over to his brother. 'I can see why you want to work there—it's a fantastic hospital.'

'Is it true that it's closing?' Lorna asked.

'Not if we can help it,' Dominic said, and from the conviction in his voice, Victoria knew that she had him fully on board now in the fight to save Paddington's.

And what were the best words in the world to hear when you've woken up having been on a stint working nights and just had really good sex?

Katie MacBride said them as Dominic put an arm around her and kissed the top of her head. 'Take a seat at the table, you two. You'll be wanting a proper dinner.'

And she was entered into his fold.

Victoria had found her family.

* * * * *

MILLS & BOON®
Hardback – April 2017

ROMANCE

The Italian's One-Night Baby	Lynne Graham
The Desert King's Captive Bride	Annie West
Once a Moretti Wife	Michelle Smart
The Boss's Nine-Month Negotiation	Maya Blake
The Secret Heir of Alazar	Kate Hewitt
Crowned for the Drakon Legacy	Tara Pammi
His Mistress with Two Secrets	Dani Collins
The Argentinian's Virgin Conquest	Bella Frances
Stranded with the Secret Billionaire	Marion Lennox
Reunited by a Baby Bombshell	Barbara Hannay
The Spanish Tycoon's Takeover	Michelle Douglas
Miss Prim and the Maverick Millionaire	Nina Singh
Their One Night Baby	Carol Marinelli
Forbidden to the Playboy Surgeon	Fiona Lowe
A Mother to Make a Family	Emily Forbes
The Nurse's Baby Secret	Janice Lynn
The Boss Who Stole Her Heart	Jennifer Taylor
Reunited by Their Pregnancy Surprise	Louisa Heaton
The Ten-Day Baby Takeover	Karen Booth
Expecting the Billionaire's Baby	Andrea Laurence

MILLS & BOON®
Large Print – April 2017

ROMANCE

A Di Sione for the Greek's Pleasure	Kate Hewitt
The Prince's Pregnant Mistress	Maisey Yates
The Greek's Christmas Bride	Lynne Graham
The Guardian's Virgin Ward	Caitlin Crews
A Royal Vow of Convenience	Sharon Kendrick
The Desert King's Secret Heir	Annie West
Married for the Sheikh's Duty	Tara Pammi
Winter Wedding for the Prince	Barbara Wallace
Christmas in the Boss's Castle	Scarlet Wilson
Her Festive Doorstep Baby	Kate Hardy
Holiday with the Mystery Italian	Ellie Darkins

HISTORICAL

Bound by a Scandalous Secret	Diane Gaston
The Governess's Secret Baby	Janice Preston
Married for His Convenience	Eleanor Webster
The Saxon Outlaw's Revenge	Elisabeth Hobbes
In Debt to the Enemy Lord	Nicole Locke

MEDICAL

Waking Up to Dr Gorgeous	Emily Forbes
Swept Away by the Seductive Stranger	Amy Andrews
One Kiss in Tokyo...	Scarlet Wilson
The Courage to Love Her Army Doc	Karin Baine
Reawakened by the Surgeon's Touch	Jennifer Taylor
Second Chance with Lord Branscombe	Joanna Neil

MILLS & BOON®
Hardback – May 2017

ROMANCE

The Sheikh's Bought Wife	Sharon Kendrick
The Innocent's Shameful Secret	Sara Craven
The Magnate's Tempestuous Marriage	Miranda Lee
The Forced Bride of Alazar	Kate Hewitt
Bound by the Sultan's Baby	Carol Marinelli
Blackmailed Down the Aisle	Louise Fuller
Di Marcello's Secret Son	Rachael Thomas
The Italian's Vengeful Seduction	Bella Frances
Conveniently Wed to the Greek	Kandy Shepherd
His Shy Cinderella	Kate Hardy
Falling for the Rebel Princess	Ellie Darkins
Claimed by the Wealthy Magnate	Nina Milne
Mummy, Nurse...Duchess?	Kate Hardy
Falling for the Foster Mum	Karin Baine
The Doctor and the Princess	Scarlet Wilson
Miracle for the Neurosurgeon	Lynne Marshall
English Rose for the Sicilian Doc	Annie Claydon
Engaged to the Doctor Sheikh	Meredith Webber
The Marriage Contract	Kat Cantrell
Triplets for the Texan	Janice Maynard

MILLS & BOON®
Large Print – May 2017

ROMANCE

A Deal for the Di Sione Ring	Jennifer Hayward
The Italian's Pregnant Virgin	Maisey Yates
A Dangerous Taste of Passion	Anne Mather
Bought to Carry His Heir	Jane Porter
Married for the Greek's Convenience	Michelle Smart
Bound by His Desert Diamond	Andie Brock
A Child Claimed by Gold	Rachael Thomas
Her New Year Baby Secret	Jessica Gilmore
Slow Dance with the Best Man	Sophie Pembroke
The Prince's Convenient Proposal	Barbara Hannay
The Tycoon's Reluctant Cinderella	Therese Beharrie

HISTORICAL

The Wedding Game	Christine Merrill
Secrets of the Marriage Bed	Ann Lethbridge
Compromising the Duke's Daughter	Mary Brendan
In Bed with the Viking Warrior	Harper St. George
Married to Her Enemy	Jenni Fletcher

MEDICAL

The Nurse's Christmas Gift	Tina Beckett
The Midwife's Pregnancy Miracle	Kate Hardy
Their First Family Christmas	Alison Roberts
The Nightshift Before Christmas	Annie O'Neil
It Started at Christmas...	Janice Lynn
Unwrapped by the Duke	Amy Ruttan

0417 GEN STD LP

MILLS & BOON®

Why shop at millsandboon.co.uk?

Each year, thousands of romance readers find their
perfect read at millsandboon.co.uk. That's because
we're passionate about bringing you the very best
romantic fiction. Here are some of the advantages
of shopping at www.millsandboon.co.uk:

* **Get new books first**—you'll be able to buy your
  favourite books one month before they hit
  the shops

* **Get exclusive discounts**—you'll also be able to buy
  our specially created monthly collections, with up
  to 50% off the RRP

* **Find your favourite authors**—latest news,
  interviews and new releases for all your favourite
  authors and series on our website, plus ideas for
  what to try next

* **Join in**—once you've bought your favourite books,
  don't forget to register with us to rate, review and
  join in the discussions

Visit **www.millsandboon.co.uk**
for all this and more today!